Public Display of Aggression

Public Display of Aggression

A novel by Hugh Fritz

Book 2 of the Mystic Rampage Series

Golden Word Books
Santa Fe, NM

Library of Congress Control Number 2020946407

Published by Golden Word Books, Santa Fe, New Mexico.

ISBN 978-1-948749-55-8

—1—

DARREN

A pair of Sport Utility Vehicles shuffled about the road. Darren Raleigh's consciousness, manifested as an invisible haze, hovered unseen above one of them and sank through the windshield. Five men were inside, survivors of a massacre he had spearheaded months ago. He didn't know the four passengers. They were merely bystanders who'd been lucky enough to escape with their lives. Darren's fury was focused on the driver, Kevin Tymbir.

"We need to stop," said one of the back seat passengers. Tymbir gripped the wheel tighter as he maneuvered through Chicago traffic. "Come on, pull over. My legs are asleep."

"And I have a headache," said the passenger in the front seat.

"And my neck is killing me," said Tymbir. "We all have problems, but I'm not stopping this car."

A crackling came from the walkie-talkie resting in the cup holder. "Tymbir, this is Clark. A request has been made that we make a pit stop." If Darren's astral projection had a face, it would have smiled as Tymbir shouted a surge of profanities into the walkie-talkie.

"We should at least stop for coffee," said Clark when Tymbir finished his rant. "There's no way I'm the only one who needs a caffeine boost." Tymbir grumbled under his breath as he parked near a Starbucks.

Darren's astral projection returned to his body, which was resting on a bench nearly a mile away. Several sheets of newspaper covered him like a blanket. As he stood up, they fell away to reveal his blue wool cap, black hoodie, and lightly tattered blue jeans. They were

1

the colors of a gang he used to be involved with, but that wasn't the part of his past he was paying tribute to. Some members had mistreated him. They'd robbed him, bullied him, and frightened his family. Whatever remained of those people was now buried under a burned down apartment building. But his time with the gang had gifted him with a few true friends. They were the ones who, along with his wife, had not deserved to die. They were the family he was honoring with his attire.

Darren retrieved one of the newspaper pages and noticed a man in a suit and tie staring at his cell phone while waiting for a bus. He waddled over and held out his hand. "Brother, can you spare a dime?" The man stared at his phone more intently and stepped to the side to put some distance between them. Darren stared at him a moment and walked away.

He found a quiet street and crouched behind a row of shrubs in front of a house. Hidden from view, he once again focused on Tymbir's car, but this time instead of performing an astral projection, he performed a summoning spell between his body and the vehicle. A moment later, he was sitting in the empty car outside the Starbucks.

He casually hopped out and walked inside, holding the newspaper high to hide his face as he made his way to the bathroom. It had been a while since he washed his clothes, and a few people gave him unhappy looks, but the important thing was to avoid being noticed by Tymbir. Clearly, he succeeded, because if Tymbir had noticed Darren, there would be a firefight right now.

The bathroom was empty. He threw away the paper, went into a stall, and closed the door. Then he sat down and lifted his shirt. A stainless steel circular blade was tied to his body by a rope running diagonally from his shoulder to his hip. It was ten inches in diameter and had once been part of an electric saw. Several of the serrated edges were dulled, and a wide hole in the flat part served as a handle. The remaining teeth would poke him periodically, especially when he sat down, but he healed quickly, so it was of no consequence. He untied the rope and set the saw blade on his lap while he waited for someone from Tymbir's group to enter. They had been driving all night and someone probably needed to use the restroom.

He didn't wait long before the door opened. In his projected form, he spied on two men from Tymbir's SUV. "Damn," one of them muttered, "no windows."

"You weren't going to do it anyway," said the other as he approached a urinal.

"I'm telling you we have to. You weren't in the house when Darren and the others came after us. We're in a battle we can't win."

"Then what's Darren been waiting for? Why haven't any of them come after us yet? They're scared of us. They should be. We've got firepower, and warrior's spirit to back it up. We'll slaughter them when they make their move."

Darren's projection returned to his body, and he smiled again. The bonds within the group were beginning to fall apart, just as he'd experience with some people he once considered friends. When the urinal flushed, he became invisible and leaned off the toilet seat. He rolled under the stall wall and used the flowing water to cover the sound he made as he crept behind the man washing his hands.

"I'm making a run for the door," said the one who'd been looking for windows. "If you're smart, you'll do the same."

"Do that and Darren will be the least of your problems. You don't want to know what my brother and I do to deserters." He bent over and splashed water on his face.

Darren stood directly behind him and became visible as he straightened his back. The man swore and spun around, throwing a punch which Darren was expecting. He blocked the man's attack and slashed his throat. The other opened his mouth to call for help, but Darren threw the blade at his chest. It sunk deep, cutting off his air as he fell. The downed man tried to reach around the saw for a gun in a shoulder holster, but Darren summoned the saw blade back to his body. The man lurched and yelped as it was torn from his ribs, and a moment later lay still. Darren retied the weapon and concealed it under his shirt. He quickly went into an alley behind the store by deconstructing a section of wall, then reconstructed it as he strode toward the busy street.

He could have gone back to the dining area and finished off Tymbir, but it wasn't the right time. Tymbir had taken everything from Darren, and to truly feel satisfied, he needed to do the same in return. Like the others in the SUV, Tymbir had already left his job and broken off all contact with his family and friends. All the team had left was each other. He would gradually pick them off until Tymbir was alone, and then he would finish him.

SOLEIL

"We're not getting anywhere," said Mohinaux as he flipped through a copy of Grimms' Fairy Tales. "I wasn't the inspiration behind all folklore. Some of these monsters are completely fictional."

Soleil shushed him and looked over his shoulder. The bookshelves were hollow, and someone could have been on the other side of the aisle.

"If you're not comfortable here, we can leave," said Mohinaux, not lowering his voice.

Soleil didn't see anyone on the other side of the shelf but double-checked by improving his hearing and listening for heartbeats. Satisfied that they were alone in the library, he slid a book across the table. "What about these? The heroes use things like swords of light and cloaks that make them invisible."

Mohinaux skimmed several pages. "Sure, I had some influence in these. Sometimes when my friends were in fights and drew their sword, I increased the temperature of the blade, making it glow red hot, which is probably where the sword of light comes from. At some point, someone must have seen me become invisible and I happened to be wearing a cloak at the time. They must have jumped to the conclusion that the fabric was magic. None of this relates to the man who attacked you at the apartment, though." Mohinaux slid the book back across the table. "Soleil, there is no fairy tale that involves a hero using spellcasting revolvers. Besides, I never used a magic gun to kill one of my monsters. I think I'd remember doing something like that."

"I'm not questioning your memory, but I think you overlooked something. Somehow the Old Ticker constructed an Enchanted object. He must have been inspired by something or someone."

"The Old Ticker?"

"We might as well start calling him something other than the man-with-the-Enchanted-guns," said Soleil. "He had a bandana wrapped around his face with an image of a clock sewn into it. Until we find out his real name, I'll be referring to him as the Old Ticker."

Mohinaux closed his book of fairy tales. "Well, I didn't overlook anything regarding these stories. I can't imagine I had anything to do with them."

Soleil picked up the book. "I'll put it back. No point in cluttering our workspace." He crossed over a few aisles and paused. After making sure nobody was watching, he sat on the floor and performed an astral projection. He knew about Darren's grudge and had been keeping an eye on Tymbir and the rest of the group. So far, nothing bad had happened to them; they just drove aimlessly around the city day and night, stopping only for food and gasoline. He hoped that over the past few months, Darren had calmed down but knew it was unlikely. Darren had loved Atalissa dearly, and when she died, he became broken and unstable. Soleil was positive that someday, Darren would strike hard at Tymbir. When that time came, he would summon his body to wherever the confrontation was taking place. He wasn't sure what he'd do then but would cross that bridge when he got to it.

He would have liked to use his powers to find Darren, but magic had complications. One issue was that spells would not work on another Genie, so astral projections were useless as a means of tracking Darren. Another was that magic spread by contact, which kept Darren from killing people in a blind rage. Tymbir would not die if Darren tried to magically break his neck or stop his heart; he would only gain a sorcerer's powers, which included rapid healing. Using magic on animals was how Mohinaux had created the mythical creatures in the books.

Soleil's projection hovered above Tymbir's vehicle near a Starbucks where a police car was parked outside and a crowd of people had gathered. He watched as Tymbir wove through the crowd with some of his team close behind. There were two fewer members than the last time Soleil had spied on them. His projection drifted inside to survey the scene. Seeing that the dining area was clean, he drifted into the bathroom and saw police officers examining the bloody remains of two men.

Soleil's projection rose through the ceiling and flew around the building like a hawk but did not spot Darren. He flew away from the Starbucks, darting a block in each direction, then two, then three, but there was still no sighting. If his projection could speak or make contact with solid objects, he would have punched a wall and shouted, but lacking the ability to do either, he returned to his body. When he opened his eyes, he was no longer alone between the two shelves. Mohinaux was standing in front of him. "You were watching Tymbir again, weren't you? We have more important things to worry about than the well-being of that hate group."

Soleil stood up and slid the book into the shelf, not caring if he'd returned it to the proper place. "The attacks have started, Dad. Two of Tymbir's friends are dead. I was too late to help them. I looked around, but Darren was already gone."

"Forget about them. Tymbir's safety isn't your responsibility."

"It's not that I want to save Tymbir," said Soleil as they returned to their table. "I want to stop Darren. You never knew him like I did. He wasn't always a killer."

"He wasn't always a Genie either," said Mohinaux. "You've lost control of the beast you created. I've been there. I'm proud of you for wanting to take responsibility for your actions, but if you want my advice, you're going about it wrong."

"What am I supposed to do?"

Mohinaux slid his thumb across his neck. "I suggest you start doing things my way."

Soleil shook his head. "Darren's a friend."

Mohinaux sighed. "That's cute, but having a positive attitude won't fix the situation. Did I ever tell you about the time I Enchanted a firefly? It became known as a Pixie. Everyone loved it. It was adorable. It was also easily spooked. When it felt threatened, it created a blinding flash. It also had a strong bite. A lot of villagers were injured, and a few died. I knew I had to get rid of it."

"Darren isn't a Pixie. He's not lashing out because he's spooked. He's after Tymbir, but he didn't kill him yet. He's building up to it. That means we have time to talk."

"Talking is fine if there's a chance of him listening." Mohinaux put a hand on Soleil's shoulder. "The bottom line is he's dangerous. It's true you're killing a friend, but you're also eliminating a threat. Focus on that."

Soleil wanted to emphasize that Darren wasn't a threat to be eliminated, but the phone in his pocket vibrated. He held his thought and answered it.

"Soleil, it's Flarence. I think we found something."

FLARENCE

Flarence stood on the roof of a motel looking at a building in the distance. He was wearing his work clothes: black dress shoes, light khaki pants, a white button-up shirt, and a gray suit jacket with excessively large pockets. One pocket contained a weapon called the Stakehail Colt, a revolver that used compressed gas to fire icicles at high enough velocity to be just as lethal as thrown knives. On his right hand was a glove with a coil gun mounted on it which consisted of a doorknob loaded into a pipe that was wrapped in wire. The doorknob was held in place with a spring, and when Flarence magically produced an electric current in the wire, the doorknob was pulled through the pipe like a piston. He called his weapon the Wrist Cannon.

On Flarence's left was Soleil, wearing a poncho patterned with red and black diamonds. Vials of poisons were held in leather pouches sewn into the center of each diamond. The severity of the poisons varied. Some were highly potent while others were only mild irritants. All the compounds had come from a single source. Years ago, Soleil had used his powers to Enchant a tree, creating the most deadly plant in the world.

Mohinaux's clothes resembled a school uniform. He wore dark pants and a white button-up shirt with information scribbled on it in permanent marker. He covered his face by fastening the straightened collar with safety pins and pulling a beanie low over his forehead until it almost touched his eyes, which were concealed behind large sunglasses. The first time Flarence saw the outfit, he hadn't known Mohinaux was the one wearing it. Under the guise of the Student, Mohinaux had kidnapped, threatened, and injured people throughout the city, which turned out to be a plan to teach Flarence a lesson about responsible use of his powers. "Is it even necessary for you to be wearing that right now?" Flarence asked. "If there's a fight, Soleil might need to use his poisons, so I can understand why he's wearing the poncho, but your shirt doesn't have any weapons on it, so what's the point?"

"The point is to maintain a particular state of mind," said Mohinaux. "You mentioned that we'd be using our powers to infiltrate a secure building, and part of preparing for that is looking the part."

"I know what you mean," said a voice behind them. The three turned around as Claire, Flarence's partner and best friend, hoisted her body onto the roof. Her hair was tied in a bun, and a pair of ten-inch steel spikes ran through its center. Her face was concealed behind a scarf with a zigzag pattern of pouches holding razor blades, and her shirt was laden with chains. She wore leather gloves with lettered rings that spelled out her nickname: R-A-Z-R on her left hand and P-U-N-K on her right. "Have you told them the plan yet?"

"He hasn't even told us what we're looking at yet," said Soleil.

"We're here because there are several bodies in that building which were found at a peculiar crime scene," said Flarence.

"We haven't had much luck finding the corpse Flarence saw come back to life in the cemetery the day he fought Darren," said Claire. "But we did stumble across something that might lead to the man you saw with the magic guns."

"Soleil has started calling him the Old Ticker," said Mohinaux.

"Because of the clock on his mask," Soleil explained after receiving confused looks from Claire and Flarence.

"The point," said Claire, "is that recently five people were found dead in a factory. The story caught my attention, and when we looked into the murders, they started showing promise."

"I used my projection to spy on the autopsy, and all the people were killed from gunshot wounds to the heart," said Flarence. "The weird thing is, there were no bullets in the bodies and no exit wounds. The investigators are in agreement that the shooter removed the bullets but can't figure out how. There's no evidence of them being surgically taken out."

"It sounds like the bullets were summoned out of the body," said Mohinaux. "This could have been Darren's work."

"We considered that option," said Claire, "but I did some research on the victims, and as far as I can tell, they have no connection with Tymbir. They were funding a young company that produces adhesives. The place will probably be shut down if the founders can't find more support soon."

"That doesn't fit the Old Ticker's profile either," said Soleil. "His last victims were gangsters living in a shabby apartment. Why would he suddenly take his anger out on entrepreneurs?"

"That's what we're here to find out," said Flarence. "I want to see what these people went through the night they were murdered. I know where the bodies are being stored, and I checked the room before you got here. It's empty except for the corpses and should be for the rest of the night. Soleil, you hold onto me and I'll summon us inside along with Razor Punk, who'll keep a lookout in the room while we work our psychometry on the deceased. Meanwhile, the Student will be our eyes outside the room." He handed a cell phone to Mohinaux. "I have Razor Punk's number on speed dial. If you see people coming, flip it open and hold down the pound key until the screen says it's dialing."

Mohinaux pocketed the phone as Soleil and Claire gripped Flarence's arms tightly. A moment later, they were standing among several metal tables, each with a body bag on it. As Flarence had promised, the room was dark and empty, and the only sound was the humming of machines working hard to recirculate the air and keep the room cold.

Flarence approached a table and unzipped the bag. "This is Marcus O'Connell. They think he died last. Since he lived the longest, I'm hoping we'll get the most out of him." He placed a hand on the dead man's shoulder, gesturing for Soleil to do the same. Claire stood close to Flarence with a razor blade in her hand. Genies lost consciousness when they performed an astral projection, and were completely un-aware of the surroundings. The psychometry spell was not quite as drastic but had similar risks. Flarence would not collapse and would retain some awareness of what was going on around him, but he would also be engrossed in the scene playing out before his eyes, as if lost in a daydream. If someone approached the room, it was Claire's job to wake Flarence by any means necessary, including cutting him.

Claire nodded and Flarence turned to Soleil, whose hand was suspended an inch above the body. Flarence grabbed his wrist and forced it onto the cold, dead flesh. "The doctors are gone for the night but security still patrols, so we need to get a move on. Ready? Three, two, one."

Flarence closed his eyes and looked into the dead man's past. A tingling sensation began at the crown of his head and spread through his body. His world became dark and silent for a moment. Then images came to him. They started as dots, which grew and took on distinctive shapes.

He was sitting in a car. Before him were the three main buildings of the Spider Web adhesive factory. One stood next to a set of train tracks which brought in raw materials. The production factory was adjacent to the receiving building, and the third was a mechanical area where vehicles and tools were taken to be repaired and stored. There was also a security booth by the parking lot and a small garage for forklifts.

The digital clock on the car's dashboard showed that it was almost ten at night. All the lights in the factory were off, no trains were coming into the receiving building, and all the forklifts were tucked away. The only light came from the security booth.

Flarence was in the passenger seat. He turned his head and saw Marcus beside him. It was snowing, but Marcus had his window down. He was smoking a cigarette and ignoring the flakes drifting onto his lap. Soon, another car approached, and Marcus flicked his half-smoked cigarette out the window before greeting the newcomers. Flarence rose to his feet, passing through the car door without opening it. What he was seeing was a replay of Marcus's last moments, so the people weren't aware of him, and objects in his way weren't really there. However, he was doing more than just peering into a memory. Flarence was glimpsing the night of Marcus's death rather than the recollection of it. He could see everything that had happened, whether or not Marcus had seen it as well.

He walked behind Marcus to the car as three people stepped out. One of them was ruffling his messy hair and seemed to be having trouble keeping his head up. Despite his tired face, he still had made an effort to look presentable by putting on a plaid shirt and tucking it into a pair of slacks. The other two were dressed more formally. A man sported a suit and tie, and a woman wore a little black dress. Flarence had seen their pictures in the news reports and recognized them as Adam and Evelyn Fisher.

"Was it really necessary to bring Charlie along?" said Marcus, gesturing to the less-formally dressed man.

"We were having dinner," said Adam. "We went a little heavy on the wine, so we needed a ride." As he took a small step forward, his shoe slid on the snow so that he stumbled into Evelyn, wrapping his arms around her for balance.

The couple giggled and straightened up as another car arrived. It parked near the rest of the group, and a man wearing tight, pressed jeans and a purple button-up shirt stepped out. Flarence recognized him as Brad, another of the victims. He stood outside his car for a moment glaring at Adam and Evelyn disapprovingly. "Where are Stuart and Gil?"

"I called them before I left to make sure they got Jason's text," said Marcus. "They said they were busy and to fill them in when the meeting is over."

"Is anyone else bothered by the fact that those two were the original founders and yet they're the ones putting the least effort into it?"

"Hey, that's why we're here," said Adam. "Those two need us to cover their backside." He slid his hand down to Evelyn's waistline. She let his hand rest there a moment before pushing away and straightening her dress.

"Does anyone know what this is about?" asked Evelyn. "Jason's message was vague."

"When I tried calling him, he didn't pick up," Marcus answered.

"Whatever it's about, let's get it over with quick," said Adam. "I really want to get home and into bed." He leaned close to Evelyn and whispered, "Not that I'm tired."

The security station was the only break in a fence that surrounded the facility. The room was split in half by a pane of glass, and the guards on duty were supposed to be at a desk behind it. When the group entered, the room was empty. "Looks like they're goofing off again," said Evelyn. "Stewart says he's found the booth empty before."

"I'll talk to them tomorrow," said Marcus.

"I'll join you," said Brad. "Did anyone bring their key card?"

"I have Mr. Fisher's card," said Charlie. He pulled it out of his pocket and ran it over the scanner. The red light turned green, and the latch clicked open.

"Who's a good little personal assistant," said Adam as he rubbed Charlie's head like he was petting a dog. Charlie's face scrunched up, but he didn't say anything. He held the door open, and the group walked through in single file.

Flarence examined the area behind the glass divider before joining them. Part of a leg was sticking out from under the desk. He ducked for a better look and saw two people in security guard uniforms hidden underneath. A dried stream of blood stained the side of their faces. They had been clubbed on the head with something very hard.

Flarence ran to catch up with the group. The five people weren't paying close attention to their surroundings, but Flarence scanned the area and noticed that they weren't alone. In the distance, standing by the tracks, a figure was watching them. From his vantage point, all Flarence could see was his white shirt and red hat. He walked toward the stranger, but as soon as the front door closed behind Marcus and the four others, the watcher disappeared. Did he summon his body somewhere? thought Flarence as he ran to the spot where the man had been.

He could see footprints in a thin layer of powder, a mix of snow and dust from the materials that came in on the train. If the stranger had used magic to travel, his body would have been lifted off the ground. He must have been running instead of summoning but too fast for Flarence to follow. A metallic sound clanked behind him, and Flarence whipped his head around to see the man wrapping a length of chain around the handles of the factory door. Then he snapped a combination lock through the links to hold it in place, and gave both the door and the lock a quick tug to make sure they were secure. Flarence tried to run to see the man better, but he was gone too quickly.

A crunching sound brought Flarence's attention to a nearby window. The stranger stood by it for a moment, then ran off again. Flarence examined the window and saw there were nails pressed into the frame, making it impossible to open. Then he saw that all the first-floor windows had been nailed shut. The stranger didn't have a hammer, which meant the nails had been pressed into the frame by hand. When Flarence looked back at the front door, the stranger was standing in front of it, looking over his handiwork before crouching low and leaping to the roof of the factory. Whatever the stranger was, he had sealed the others inside. Flarence passed through the wall and caught up with the group.

The first floor contained vats and mixing machines that were turned off. The building was empty with the exception of Marcus and his friends who were standing in front of an elevator. Adam gingerly took hold of Evelyn's wrist. He swayed back and forth with each passing second. She giggled as she matched his movements, clicking her tongue to mimic a clock. There was a ding as the doors opened, and Flarence made it inside with the group just as they closed again. The second floor was much different, carpeted, with cubicles and computers. Clearly, this was the business area. Marcus and his friends walked through the room to an office at the far end. Charlie entered first and held the door for the rest of them but then stopped short, leaving the door half open.

Brad pushed past him into the office. "Get a move on, kid. What's wrong with you?" The moment he was in the room, he stopped as well. "Shit!" he swore as his hand slapped against his chest.

Flarence passed through them and saw someone sitting limp in a leather chair behind an oak desk. His head hung uselessly, and a ring of dried blood stained his shirt.

"I'll call nine-one-one," said Charlie. But the moment he took his phone out, there was a pop, and the device was thrown from his hand. Everyone, including Flarence, spun to see what had knocked the phone away, but the room appeared to be empty. Charlie approached his phone and saw that it was smashed. As he examined it, something emerged from the screen and flew out of the room. Flarence didn't know what the others were thinking, but he thought the object looked like a bullet.

Marcus picked up the phone on Jason's desk. "There's no dial tone."

Flarence figured the stranger in the red hat must have taken care of that after sealing the group inside.

"Let's get out of here," said Evelyn. The five of them ran back to the elevator, Adam and Evelyn stumbling a little because of their drinks. They stopped when they saw the man from outside standing in front of the elevator doors.

Now Flarence got his first good look at him. He was wearing steel-toed work boots, blue jeans, and a red baseball cap. His face was hidden by a red rag that extended to his chin, an upper band tied around his head and lower band tied under his ears to hold it in place. Two eyeholes cut into it revealed a cold, glassy stare. Tufts of stiff, wiry hair jutted out of the sides of his hat. He was wearing nitrile gloves and held a wooden stick that looked like it had been broken off from a mop or a broom. The white shirt Flarence thought he was wearing was actually a lab coat over a red T-shirt. On the right side of the coat, a name tag said R.E.D. On the left side, above the stranger's heart, was a dark stain.

Nobody said anything for a moment. The stranger simply stared at the five others. Charlie looked terrified and confused, while everyone else just looked terrified. Finally, Adam was able to speak a single word: "Roy?"

"That name brings back painful memories," Roy said in a gravelly voice. "For calling me that, you're first." He threw the wooden stick like a spear at Adam's thigh.

Adam screamed and fell to one knee, grasping the stick that had impaled him. Evelyn bent next to him and tried to help him up, but he was too heavy and her grip slipped. Charlie and Marcus were running. Brad grabbed Evelyn's arm and dragged her away. "Adam!" she called as she tried to go to him, but Brad's hold was too tight.

Flarence watched as Roy took hold of the wooden stick and twisted it deeper, making Adam scream to the point where Flarence was surprised he didn't pass out from the pain. Then Roy swung it like a hockey stick, pulling it from Adam's leg and sending him rolling across the floor. "Roy," he managed to say through choking sobs, "please don't. I'm sorry."

"Apologies are in order, but yours is not accepted," said Roy as he dropped the stick and grabbed Adam by the neck. He lifted him up with one hand and pinned him against a wall so their hearts were aligned. "Anything else to say?" Adam only coughed. "Bleed as I bled." A barrage of black shards erupted from Roy's chest into Adam's, whose final screams were choked short as his body twitched and went limp in Roy's grasp. The shards exited Adam's chest and returned to Roy's before he let go and followed in the direction of Marcus and his friends.

Flarence ran past Roy to catch up with the group. If he wasn't so worried about being interrupted, he'd freeze the vision to get a closer look at Roy. For now, he felt it was more important to watch as much of the night as he could. Roy seemed to like talking before striking. Perhaps he'd reveal useful information.

Marcus was the first to the front door, but the chains held it in place regardless of how much he struggled to force it open. Evelyn had stopped trying to go back to Adam, but her eyes were wet and her cheeks flushed. Brad held her and tried to comfort her while Charlie ran to the nearest window and struggled with it as Marcus struggled with the door.

"Oh God," said Evelyn, "the letter. We're all going to die."

"We're not going to die," said Brad. "I don't know what's going on here but that isn't him."

"It's him," said Evelyn. "He's back. He's coming for us."

"He isn't going to get us," said Marcus, pulling out his cell phone. "I'll call the cops. Brad, find something we can use to break the windows."

Brad picked up a metal bucket that was catching drippings from an overhead pipe. He dumped the liquid on the floor and swung the bucket at a window.

Roy appeared in front of him, moving at his too-fast-to-follow speed. He caught the bucket before it struck the window pane. Marcus was frantically providing his location over the phone and begging the police officer at the other end to send help quickly. A piece of metal burst from Roy's chest and flew to Marcus's phone, knocking it out of his hand. A moment later, it leaped from the phone back to Roy's chest. Brad cocked his arm and threw a punch, putting all his weight into it, but Roy was not fazed. Marcus bellowed as he continued the assault, but Roy's head barely moved as Brad's fist connected with his jaw.

Roy crumpled the bucket like paper and struck Brad below his ribs with it. Charlie, Marcus, and Evelyn ran as Roy gripped a handful of Brad's hair and lifted him by it, then struck Brad in the face with the bucket before tossing it across the room. "Revenge is a bitch," said Roy as Brad hung limp and suspended with his bloodied face. Roy moved Brad so their hearts were aligned: "It's time to bleed as I bled." Again, a cluster of black shards burst from Roy's chest and struck Brad in his. "Three down, two to go."

Flarence recalled Roy's last words to Adam. It had been a rhyme. As he ran after the others, he mouthed what Roy had said to Brad and counted the syllables. It was a haiku.

Charlie, Marcus, and Evelyn were at another exit where the door was jammed like the other. "It's no good," said Charlie. "Whoever that guy is he's locked us in."

"It's Roy," said Evelyn. "We killed him."

"Guys, what's going on?" said Charlie.

"We thought we were just going to rough him up and scare him off," said Marcus.

"We didn't know how much this company meant to Stuart and Gil," said Evelyn. "We had no idea how far they'd go to protect it."

"But you were all there," said Roy, who had caught up with them. Marcus tried to run. Roy pushed him into a wall. As Evelyn tried to run, Roy grabbed her by the hair and threw her to the floor. He turned to Charlie, who was frozen in fear. "You're the one person I won't stop if you try to run." Charlie's knees were shaking and he stood still, too afraid to move. "Fine," said Roy, "stay and watch."

"Four shots to the heart" said Marcus. "You were gone."

"You're still having doubts?" said Roy. "In case you haven't figured it out yet, that letter really was from me."

Evelyn came at Roy from behind and threw her hands around his neck, trying to strangle him. He grabbed her wrists and pushed off the floor with his foot, sending them both flying across the room until her back crashed into a metal cabinet so she was sandwiched between Roy and the hard steel. He continued pushing with his feet, applying more pressure as he crushed her against the cabinet. Evelyn's screams turned to gasps as her ribs cracked and the air was forced out of her lungs. He effortlessly lifted her over his head and dropped her to the floor, then grabbed her arms and threw her across the room where she landed slumped against the wall. Then Roy turned his attention to Marcus and Charlie. "It's just down to you two now." They ran. Roy turned to Evelyn who was coughing and squirming on the floor.

"It's time to join your husband and your friend. Now don't try to get up. Bleed as I bled."

Flarence stopped dwelling on the rhymes. He found it to be an interesting habit, but that's all it was. It didn't seem to reveal anything about Roy's motivation. Charlie's questioning had been much more enlightening. He turned away from Evelyn before Roy struck her down with his metal shards, eager to catch up with the others.

Charlie was having trouble keeping up with Marcus. They nearly collided when Marcus stopped short and put a finger over his mouth. In the distance they could hear Roy's boots on the floor. The storage room they were in contained rows of tall shelves filled with crates containing bags of materials used to make the adhesive. Marcus went around a shelf and Charlie followed him. They stayed quiet and watched through a gap in the crates as Roy walked by. "What's going on?" Charlie whispered after Roy had passed them and his footsteps grew faint.

"Gil shot him," said Marcus.

"You need to give me more than that."

"Look, it's hard to get a new company started. Roy got in our way. We went to talk to him, but things got out of hand and Gil wound up pulling a trigger. We thought the guy was done for, but a few days ago, we each received a letter." He pulled a folded piece of paper out of his pocket. Charlie unfolded and read it but said nothing. Flarence examined the letter over Charlie's shoulder.

"I assumed someone saw us kill Roy and was trying to screw with us or blackmail us," Marcus explained.

"Your first thought would be blackmail."

Charlie and Marcus looked up and saw Roy standing on top of a shelving unit with a plastic bag in each hand. They were labeled with long words which Flarence assumed he'd understand better if he had an interest in chemistry. Roy hurled the bags to the floor. They burst, engulfing Charlie and Marcus in fine powder. Charlie dropped the letter and the two tried to escape from the cloud, but the material had made the floor slippery and they both fell.

Roy stepped off the shelves and landed in front of Marcus who tried to stand but was still having trouble balancing. "Your fate is far worse than jail," Roy said as he pinned Marcus to the ground. "It's time to bleed as I bled."

The shards erupted from his chest and Marcus lay still in the white powder, slowly staining it red as the blood oozed from his body. Marcus convulsed for a moment, then let out his last breath. Charlie was petrified with fear. Roy brought the metal shards back into his body and rose to his feet. "Two more left to end," he said as he ran off, leaving only a trail of footprints on the factory floor. There was a crash in the distance as Roy slammed his body into the front door hard enough to snap the chain that had held it closed. After he collected himself, Charlie ran out as fast as he could, leaving the letter, powder spill, and bodies as they were.

Flarence stood alone over Marcus's body and considered what he had seen before he brought himself out of the vision. When he opened his eyes, Soleil and Claire were standing by the door, and in the distance he could hear shouting and banging. Soleil had a vial of poison in each hand while Claire held a needle in one hand and a razor blade in the other.

"What's going on?" said Flarence.

"He's awake!" Soleil shouted. The distant commotion suddenly stopped, and Soleil vanished from the room. Claire sprinted to Flarence and said "cafe."

Flarence grabbed her by the shoulders and summoned his body out of the room, dragging her along as he flew to Soleil's Cafe. They landed by the counter in the restaurant, where Soleil and Mohinaux were waiting for them. "That wasn't the plan," he said. "We weren't supposed to draw attention."

"I wanted to wake you, but Soleil insisted I shouldn't," said Claire.

"I chickened out early," said Soleil. "I watched Adam's death and didn't want to see any others. I considered waking you up when we heard the security guards but then figured knowing as much as we could about Roy was more important than avoiding being seen, especially if he's going to kill more people. I called Dad and told him to keep the guards distracted."

"What did you find out?" asked Mohinaux. "Was it the Old Ticker that killed them?"

"No," said Flarence, "it was the corpse. He's more dangerous than we thought, and it sounded like the murders were personal."

"Did you learn enough to track him through your astral projections?" asked Claire.

"Maybe," said Flarence. "He's definitely supernatural. I'm not sure if astral projections will work on him. But I know the names of his next targets." He turned to Soleil. "Razor Punk and I will handle this. You and the Student keep looking for the Old Ticker. We'll meet here tomorrow and brief each other on what we know." Soleil nodded and Flarence held his hand out to Claire, but pulled it back before she grasped it. "Get me some paper."

Soleil went upstairs and came back down with a sheet of lined paper which Flarence took and folded into quarters.

"I also need to borrow your red pen," he said to Mohinaux who gave him a pen from his shirt pocket. Flarence unfolded the paper and copied the five lines he had seen on Marcus's letter.

You knew me as Inspector R.E.D.
Thanks to you painful dreams plague my head
You filled my heart with lead
But I'm back from the dead
And now you will bleed as I bled

He focused on the ink and moved it around until it copied the spacing and handwriting exactly as he'd seen it. He then took Claire's hand and summoned his body to their hotel. "It's getting late and we should get some sleep. I'll fill you in on the details of what Inspector R.E.D. can do tomorrow. He isn't human, but I don't think he's a Genie either. He's going after the last two owners of the company, so we'll have to pay them a visit."

—2—

DARREN

He watched and waited for his opportunity to kill again. The group usually stuck to the city, but after the death of two members, the others decided to leave Chicago altogether. It didn't matter where they went. He would hunt them down and kill them all. Leaving the city was just Tymbir trying new things to feel like he was in control of the situation. Darren would enjoy sending a message to make it painfully clear that Tymbir was in control of nothing.

The group had decided to go west, and its vans were moving steadily down the highway late at night. They had left the city behind miles ago, and now there was nothing but fields of corn on either side of the road. There were no rest stops around, and few other cars. Darren summoned his body to a spot near the road and walked to a ditch near the highway where he once again spied on the vans, prepared to strike when they were close.

Darren's projection watched from miles away as a tire on one of the vans burst. The vehicle swerved but the driver regained control and pulled over, the second van stopping close behind. The rumbling of the engines ceased but the headlights stayed on as everyone stepped out, some of them holding guns and probably suspecting Darren was behind the incident. Five of them spread out to stand guard while Tymbir and two others examined the blown-out tire. Darren's projection drifted close to the van and saw that the tire had not been punctured. A portion of it was melted.

Tymbir told the others to stay alert as he got the spare tire. The gunmen scanned the area with their flashlights while Darren's projection surveyed the scene and saw someone else on the side of the road with a gun of his own. Darren had seen the man before. Not too long ago, the man had tried to kill him and Soleil. His shirt was decorated with strange symbols, and his face was hidden by a bandana with an image of a clock on it. His guns somehow had the ability to cast spells, and could be used on a living person without Enchanting them; they could even be used on Genies. The last time Darren had been hit by the man's spellcasting revolver, it had electrocuted him. The shock would have been fatal if not for his magically enhanced durability and healing. Seeing the guns in action gave Darren an idea of how they worked: The man cycled through the revolvers' six chambers by pressing a switch on the grip with his thumb, and each chamber fired a different spell. Darren recalled witnessing the electrocution and burn spells.

The mystery man's motives were unclear, but for some reason, he had apparently targeted Tymbir. He fired his spellcasting revolver at one of the men standing guard, making the snow at his feet freeze solid and encase his shoes in a layer of ice. For a moment, the man struggled to get free as his lips and skin quickly turned blue. He would have collapsed but the snow falling on his body also froze and encased him in a layer of ice that held him upright. The masked assailant ran to the frozen man as Tymbir's team returned fire, their bullets shattering parts of the frozen body, but enough of a shield was left to provide a moment of cover.

Darren's projection returned to his body. He rose to his feet, drew the saw blade, and summoned his body to one of the vans. When he arrived, he ran around the frozen gunman and threw the blade. The stranger clicked the thumb switch to rotate the cylinder a few degrees, and when he fired, the blade turned into a pile of metal dust which fell harmlessly to the ground. *Deconstruction,* Darren mentally noted. *Freezing.* Two more abilities. He reconstructed the blade, summoned it back to his body, and charged as the stranger selected a different chamber. Darren held the blade above his head and swung down, aiming for the Χ symbol on the man's chest. He fired and rolled out of the way as Darren felt every muscle in his body tense and was overcome with pain followed by numbness as he fell, hitting his head against what remained of the frozen man. It was the electrocution spell again. He was getting sick of being hit with that one.

Darren's attack had missed, but when the man rolled out of the way, he was exposed to Tymbir's group, and a bullet grazed his thigh. Though not seriously hurt, he fell before he could shoot another spell. He scrambled across the road to avoid more bullets, and rolled down a slope at the side of the highway. Darren followed him.

"You're not on my list," said the gunman when Darren landed nearby. "Why are you after me?"

Darren would have responded, but blood burst from his head as a bullet struck his temple. The masked gunman fired an electrocution spell at the shooter. Darren slowly rose to his feet and shook his head as the man drew a second revolver.

"Maybe we can help each other. Let's kill some more of these folks tomorrow night. I'll see you then." He pointed the gun to his head, pulled the trigger, and disappeared. He summoned himself somewhere, thought Darren. That's ability number five. He had drawn the second gun to do it, though. Together, the two guns might have a range of twelve abilities. There were more popping noises, and Darren felt a burst of pain in his back as he was hit with more bullets. He stood still and took the hits until the gunmen were out of ammo, then walked up the hill clutching the saw blade hard enough to make his knuckles pale. The group ran to the van without the blown-out tire and clambered in. "You'd better run," Darren shouted as the engine revved up and the driver bolted down the snowy highway as fast as he could without losing control. Darren turned to the abandoned van and summoned the bullets in his body to it. When he healed, he made his way to a nearby barn, crept inside, and found a place to rest for the night.

SOLEIL

The heat on his face made him open his eyes, and he breathed deeply, enjoying the earthy aroma. His cafe was also his house, the bottom floor being the dining area and the top floor everything else. The small room upstairs was just large enough for a bed and dresser, with a door leading to the bathroom. The bedroom was packed with a variety of house plants, and he had installed extra windows to give them enough light to grow, and to also let the sun be his alarm clock.

After a quick shower, he went downstairs but didn't open the cafe. Instead he ran his hand under the counter where he had stored a plastic bag of leaves, berries, petals, and bark scrapings from his Enchanted tree. He opened a drawer under the counter where he kept the utensils to prepare his poisons, then filled a small pot with water, and put it on the stove to boil. Then he turned on his portable radio, put on a pair of disposable gloves, and got to work.

As Billy Joel's "We Didn't Start the Fire" played on an oldies station, Soleil took some leaves from the plastic bag, diced them with a knife, and put the fragments in a mesh ball tea infuser which he dropped into the water. As the leaves soaked, he dropped the bark into a porcelain mortar and ground it with a pestle into a fine powder. Then he placed an empty vial on a metal rack which held it upright, folded a cloth napkin and rolled it into a cone, and positioned it over the vial. Using an aluminum spatula, he directed the bark into the opening. When he'd scooped as much as he could into the vial, he took a bottle of olive oil from the refrigerator and poured some into a graduated cylinder.

The ability to perform deconstruction and reconstruction spells made the fluid a reservoir of solvents. He knew from experimenting that the bark contained a toxin that was most effectively extracted with esters. Soleil broke and reformed the chemical bonds, rearranging the oxygen, hydrogen, and carbon, then transferred the modified solution to the vial with the bark before moving on to the berries. Once again, he manipulated the olive oil, this time forming an alcohol, and used it to fill two vials about halfway. He dropped the berries into the alcohol and used the spatula to crush them and extract the juice. When the liquid was a satisfying dark blue, he capped the vials, inverted them a few times, and set them on the rack with the vial of powdered bark.

Most of the poisons Soleil used consisted of liquids or powders. Recently, however, he had decided he needed a weapon that was more direct. He had bought a set of stainless steel-tipped darts with brass barrels, aluminum shafts, and bright yellow flights which he thought looked cool. He removed the darts from their cases and a twig covered in leaves that resembled pine needles from a plastic bag. Then he deconstructed sections of the dart tips to make cavities running along the length that were just large enough to fit the needles inside. By the time he was done, the water was boiling and the leaves in the infuser had given the tea a dark orange-red color. He turned off the stove and emptied the infuser into the napkin he had used as a funnel earlier. Then he took off his gloves, got a slice of bread from the refrigerator, and went outside.

He wandered into the forest, staying away from the paved trail which bikers and joggers tended to use in the morning. There was some snow on the ground from a flurry the previous night, but the weather was known to change erratically, and at the moment, it was surprisingly warm. He dropped the bread by a tree and waited. It wasn't long before a squirrel approached and nibbled at it. As it ate, Soleil whipped the dart at the animal, striking one of its hind legs. The squirrel shrieked and bolted up a tree as the dart fell out of its leg. Soleil rushed to the tree and looked up to see the effects of the poison. The squirrel ran back and forth on a branch, screaming loudly and stopping once in a while to scratch violently at the bark. Suddenly, the squirrel stopped, wobbled a little, and fell off the branch. Soleil approached it cautiously. One leg was still twitching, and he poked the animal with a stick. It did not get up. Soon the twitching stopped, and he moved closer for an inspection. The squirrel looked like it had been rabid, its eyes bloodshot and saliva around its mouth.

When he returned to the cafe, the leaves were dry and the water cool. He folded the napkin, took it outside, and went to the back of the cafe where he climbed a ladder to the roof and placed the napkin near his sundial. He heated the fabric until it burst into flames and the ashes scattered in the wind. Burning the leaves broke down the poisons and rendered them harmless.

Soleil decided to check on Tymbir. Things had changed. Now there was only one van, with fewer people in it. Darren must have attacked again recently. Soleil had missed his chance to interfere. His projection returned to his body as Mohinaux's advice echoed in his mind—that killing Darren was the best option. He had only considered his father's words for a moment before images of Darren were replaced by memories of Tyrell. He performed another astral projection to confirm that Tyrell was alone and then summoned his body to the townhouse where he was living.

It was not an impressive place but was an improvement over the dormitory. The space there hadn't been bad, but Tyrell went to bed early and preferred quiet while his roommate stayed up late and played loud music. A discussion of the issue ended with Tyrell being pushed over and having his wheelchair thrown out the window. No one was hurt because the room was on the first floor, but in spite of begging his roommate to get the chair, Tyrell eventually had to crawl outside to retrieve it himself.

It didn't take long for word of what happened to spread, and while Tyrell's friends were willing to stand up for him, he was still uncomfortable sharing space with his roommate. Being a dedicated student, he spent a lot of time seeking tutoring outside of class and was close to a few teaching assistants. One of them was studying abroad and had asked Tyrell to stay at his townhouse while he was gone. Tyrell accepted the house-sitting, gaining freedom from dormitory life for the rest of the year.

As usual, he was studying alone when Soleil appeared. "How's Dad?" he asked. "Is he still . . . ."

"He's still alive," said Soleil.

"Does that mean you know where he is?" said Tyrell.

"No, I just know where he's been. Several of Tymbir's remaining friends have been killed in the past two days. If I don't get the chance to talk to him soon, he might kill every last one of them. It's not an ideal scenario, but at least he'll finally be done with all this. He's not the only problem, though. Things have actually gotten crazier." He told Tyrell about what he and Flarence had seen of Inspector R.E.D., and that he still had made no progress with the Old Ticker.

"The Old Ticker?" said Tyrell. "Because of his mask? I like it." He rolled away from the table and pulled a laptop out of his backpack. "I've been thinking about that guy actually. I might have stumbled across something useful." He powered on the device and after a few clicks handed it to Soleil. The information was dry and boring and Soleil hadn't gotten halfway through before looking up. "Is this one of your textbooks?"

"It's not a required book," said Tyrell. "I just have a thing for this stuff. It seems like you should too. Come on, you don't see it?"

Soleil turned his attention back to the screen and let his eyes wander around the page. A moment passed before two characters caught his attention: W+. "The Old Ticker had a symbol on his glove that looked like the letter W with a plus sign over it."

"Exactly," said Tyrell. "The book explains things called bosons. From what I understand, they're sort of like mediators of forces. The charged W and neutral Z bosons are part of something called the weak force. There are other bosons as well. Gravitons haven't been discovered yet, but they're hypothetical regulators of gravity. The lambda symbol is used in equations to represent the wavelength of photons which, according to this book, are another kind of boson. I'm guessing the X refers to X-rays, which are photons with very short wavelengths."

Soleil swiped his finger across the screen. "What about his mask?"

Tyrell shrugged. "I'm not sure about that one. I can't even begin to imagine how his guns work. All I can say is the symbols on his clothes are similar to the symbols used in this line of research. I don't know anything about using bosons to regulate temperature, but that doesn't mean it isn't possible. As long as you and Mohinaux are stumped, I'll keep looking into it."

"You don't have to do that," said Soleil. "We can look into it ourselves." He looked at Tyrell's legs. "I don't want you getting hurt even worse."

"I'm just going to do some internet searches. If the Old Ticker's a quantum physicist, research is going to be more useful than magic, and I've never seen you touch a computer. Do you even have a phone?"

"I kept the one Brittany gave me. How's she doing, by the way?"

"I wouldn't know. We don't keep in touch. I can't really blame her."

An awkward silence followed as the memories flooded back to them. It became overbearing, until Soleil broke the silence. "I'll follow your dad for as long as it takes, and I won't be late again. I'll watch Tymbir in my projected form all night if I have to, and the second Darren shows up, I'll be there." The two talked for a while longer before Soleil summoned his body back to the cafe. When he arrived, Mohinaux was there, staring at the door and looking like he was preparing for a fight. "What are you doing here?" asked Soleil.

"I thought I'd stop by and check in on you," said Mohinaux. "There's someone out there."

Soleil tiptoed to a window and peeked outside, where he saw a man and a woman. "Customers!" he said as he rushed to the counter and hid the poisons and glassware he had prepared earlier.

"This place gets customers?" said Mohinaux.

"Once in a blue moon, someone decides to try the place out and see if it's any good. Quick, try to look presentable." Soleil paused when he realized Mohinaux was wearing his white shirt with notes scribbled on it. "Either change or get out of here." He heard the footsteps moving away and rushed to the door, flinging it open before the couple got too far. "Sorry about the delay," he called. "I'm open. I'm just having a bit of a late start. Give me a minute." He went back into the cafe and saw that Mohinaux was still in the room and still wearing his Student shirt, chuckling as he leaned against the counter. "Dad, seriously," said Soleil as he placed the chairs on the floor and straightened the salt and pepper shakers on the tables. "I know this place doesn't look like much, but I enjoy working here. Please, help me out." When there was no response, Soleil turned and realized he was talking to himself. He saw that the napkin dispensers were all full, and returned to the door, handing the two customers menus and apologizing again for the delay as they walked in.

FLARENCE

Research on the Spider Web adhesive company revealed that it had been started by two brothers, Gil and Stewart Saucen. Digging further into their lives showed that they belonged to a wealthy family and had inherited a large sum from their grandparents. Apparently, they'd used the money to start Spider Web, although why they chose adhesives was a mystery. Claire had pieced together the establishment of the factory and the complications that came with it.

The brothers, while clearly ambitious, did not seem to have much business sense, and construction was reported to have stalled several times. Gil and Stewart burned through their inheritance quickly, and for a time, it looked like the factory was not going to be completed. But the dream was saved when the brothers received support from a group of investors. It didn't come as a surprise to Flarence that the investors were Marcus, Evelyn, Brad, Jason, and Adam.

Flarence and Claire wanted to keep an eye on the Saucen brothers together, but that was not an option. While Stewart continued to show up for work, Gil apparently had been spooked by the letter and gone into hiding. He was staying at a farmhouse with a woman who was either a romantic interest or a friend. Once his astral projection found Gil, Flarence brought Claire to the farm and then summoned his body to Stewart's office. He didn't like leaving her on her own, but she had survived fights with Genies before. If she could defend herself from someone with the ability to perform summoning spells and manipulate gravity, she could defend herself from something with super speed and strength.

Some of the factory's departments were allowed only limited operation so police could investigate the murders. The company still had orders to fill, though, and Stewart met with the supervisors of each section first thing in the morning to go over quotas that had been increased to make up for the lost time, which meant his office would be vacant for a while. Flarence quickly searched the papers in the desk but couldn't find anything dealing with a man named Roy. When there was nothing left to search, he passed the time by folding Post-it notes into triangles and flicking them into a waste basket on the other side of the room.

When Stewart returned, Flarence had gone through an entire pad of Post-its; fewer than half had made it into the basket. Stewart was carrying a folder stuffed with papers under his arm, which he almost dropped at the sight of a stranger in his office. Flarence picked up the yellow triangles scattered on the floor and took them back to the desk to try again. "Stewart Saucen, hi. Don't be shy. Come on in. My name's Flarence."

Stewart hesitated. He stood still and let the door slowly close behind him. "I'm sorry, did we have an appointment? You're not wearing a visitor's badge. Are you with the police?"

"I'm a private investigator looking into the murders. I'm here on Charlie's behalf."

"Can I see some identification?" said Stewart.

"Sorry, I don't carry business cards," said Flarence. "My area of expertise isn't usually portrayed in a positive light."

"Look, I don't know who you are, but if you have an interest in what happened, either show me a badge or watch the news. I've already told the cops everything I know."

"I highly doubt you told the cops everything about why they died."

"There wasn't much to tell. I wasn't at the factory that night, so it's not like I saw what happened."

"Did you tell them about the letter?" Flarence showed his copy of the note. "Did you tell them about Inspector R.E.D?"

Stewart stared at the paper. "The police found a letter like that at the crime scene. I told them I didn't know what it meant."

"But you know exactly what it means. It refers to a man named Roy, who your brother killed."

Stewart shut the blinds on the windows by the office door. "You don't know what you're talking about."

"Believe me, I know. Like I said, I'm here on Charlie's behalf. My frowned-upon area of expertise is paranormal crime scenes. Charlie heard about what you did to Roy. He couldn't tell me why it happened, though."

Stewart leaned against the door and rubbed a hand over his face. With a sigh, he came undone, eager to release the information he'd been holding inside. "Gil and I reached out to a consultant named Roy Elburn Davis. He said everyone called him Inspector R.E.D. on account of his initials. We hired him to make sure things at the factory were up to code and in compliance with regulations. We weren't. At least not on everything. I never hurt him, though."

Flarence tore his attention away from the Post-its and looked at Stewart. "You're safe here. I already know you were involved with Roy's death, and I didn't convey that information to the cops. I promise that everything said in this room stays between us."

Stewart sighed and continued. "Roy compiled a list of recommendations and returned periodically to look at our progress. One of his suggestions regarded our handling and storage of waste to prevent it from leaching into the ground. He also did a very thorough inspection of our production process and told us our employees were being exposed to high concentrations of volatile chemicals. We took some steps to improve the conditions, but Roy came back, ran more tests on the air quality and collected soil and water samples, and the results weren't very good."

"He never shut the factory down, in spite of the problems he saw?"

"He didn't jump to that option right away," explained Stewart. "He could easily have sent a report to other people who could fine us and possibly close the plant, but first, he tried to work with us. After all, for all the problems he found, this place wasn't exactly a death trap. The issues weren't urgent but could be problematic in the future. Brad and I had long conversations with him about ways to improve the factory, but money was always a problem. We had to go for the least expensive solutions possible, and what we did was never good enough.

"To make matters worse, some employees started complaining about the conditions. They worked long hours, and some of them were reporting health problems that they blamed on chemicals they were exposed to. Gil reached out to a temp agency which solved our low employment issue but also brought problems of its own. The new workers were inexperienced, and there was a language barrier which made training difficult. Accidents happened. The injuries the new workers were experiencing, along with the results of the soil and water tests and the investigations into the previous workers who complained about health problems, made Roy more aggressive."

"Is that when you killed him?" asked Flarence.

"I didn't kill him! I tried talking to him. I explained that we were doing our best to make the factory as good as possible, but he said he was sick of dealing with us. He said that he'd been patient with our slow progress but it was one thing after another around here, and it was time for more decisive action. Gil tried to bribe him but Roy knew our funds were nearly depleted and that the check wouldn't clear."

"So Roy turned down your bribe, and then you killed him?"

Stewart wobbled and Flarence got up to let him sit at the desk. "It wasn't supposed to be that way. Gil arranged a meeting. He brought me, Brad, Evelyn, Adam, and Jason together and convinced us that Roy was going to bring the company down. By this time, we had some ideas to improve the factory conditions. Gil told us that all we needed was a clean slate and then everything would be fine, but we needed to make sure Roy didn't bother us anymore.

"We knew Roy took his job seriously and had a room nearby. It used to be a video store, but it closed down and Roy rented the space so he could work close to us. We were just going to rough him up a little, threaten him, and get rid of his records. We raided his room, tore up the papers, and smashed his computer along with any external memory units he had. That was supposed to be the end. We told him to stay away from our factory. We felt that our point was made and were on our way out when all of a sudden Gil pulled out a gun. Apparently, he felt Roy needed to be silenced permanently."

Flarence placed his hands on the desk and leaned toward Stewart. "Gil failed. Roy is definitely the one who killed your partners. Where's the space he rented? I'd like to check it out." Stewart was silent, reluctant to give him the information. "Roy is trying to kill you," Flarence pressed. "I can either keep an eye on you and your brother all day and night until he shows up, or I can try to track him down and stop him before he comes after you." He retrieved a Post-it, unfolded it, and brought it to Stewart who scribbled down the address. Flarence left and called Claire as soon as he was outside the factory. "Are you hurt?" he asked the moment she answered.

"I'm fine, Flarence. There's no sign of Inspector R.E.D., and it's been boring watching Gil and his girlfriend. They've done nothing but eat and have sex all morning."

"I'm pretty sure Stewart is safe for the moment. I'll keep an eye on him with my astral projections every now and then, but if the last murders are any indication, Inspector R.E.D. likes waiting for night and isolating his victims before attacking. I'm going to check a place out. If he shows up, call me immediately. We don't know the full extent of his powers."

Flarence went to the address Stewart had given him. It was a small building with most of the windows blocked by cardboard. There was no sign indicating the space was for rent. Flarence considered using magic to get inside but decided to try the door first. Its rusty hinges resisted, but it was unlocked. The building was empty. The floor was dusty but there was no blood, no signs of a struggle, no evidence that a murder had ever taken place there. Flarence placed his palm on the floor and looked into the building's past. He saw Stewart and the other partners raid the room and destroy Roy's belongings, and then saw Gil fire the gun. The group panicked and left quickly, but someone must have heard the shot and called the police. Roy was still alive when help arrived; Gil had narrowly missed his heart. Flarence couldn't see the ambulance outside the building but heard the paramedics say where they were taking the body.

Scenes flashed by quickly. An investigation was conducted. The space was photographed and evidence was collected. Soon, Roy returned. The same day Flarence fought him in the cemetery, he stumbled into the room bewildered and terrified. He sulked alone for a while but was scared off when investigators came to look at the building again. They returned from time to time, but Roy did not.

There was not enough information to guess where Roy was at the moment, but Flarence had enough to continue his search. The hospital Roy had been taken to the night he was shot was likely the place Darren had collected the body. Flarence moved the dust around to hide his footprints and went to the hospital.

—3—

DARREN

Usually, feeling his weapon was comforting, but as he placed his hand on top of his shirt and caressed the serrated edge underneath, even that didn't bring any ease. Everything felt different this time. For one thing, Darren wasn't in Chicago anymore. After being attacked, the group of gunmen had continued west and finally stopped in the small town of DeKalb.

At first, it seemed like a small, quiet place that was perfect for a few brutal murders followed by a quick getaway, but the town was the site of a university campus. The streets weren't nearly as active as the city's, though there were still people out and about. Not only was the campus an inconvenience but it also got Darren thinking about his son. Every once in a while, he wanted to visit Tyrell, but he felt that it would do more harm than good. It had been hard enough for Tyrell to accept having a gangster for a father while he was growing up; accepting that his father had become a supernatural killing machine seemed like too much to ask. Darren's life was now entirely devoted to killing Tymbir. He didn't have any plan about what to do next, which was part of the reason he was dragging out his mission for so long.

He put Tyrell out of his mind and focused on the task at hand. As usual, he was watching them from a distance. Upon arriving in DeKalb, Tymbir and his friends had checked into a motel, then spent the day wandering around and talking until they found a wide open field. It wasn't a stadium, but yard markers were painted on the grass for the football team to practice.

It seemed like they were finally beginning to notice the principles of Darren's powers. They knew enough to keep their distance from large objects that he could summon his body to. Their car, which Darren had used as a summoning object, was parked in a gravel lot a long way from the field. They also knew Darren could become invisible but not intangible, which meant that if he approached across the field, someone might see his feet disturbing the snow. They still didn't know what it took to kill him—even Darren didn't know—but they knew that bullets could at least slow him down. However, Darren had not seen them restock their bullets, so they might be running low on ammo, and after so long on the road, they were likely running out of money as well. Darren gleefully imagined a future in which Tymbir was defenseless, penniless, and friendless.

He reached under his shirt and took out the saw blade. The stranger from last night said he would meet him, but Darren did not plan on waiting. He didn't trust the man, didn't know why he was trying to kill Tymbir, and didn't even know how the stranger was tracking them. Darren took a few steps toward the field but was stopped when he felt a hand on his shoulder. He spun around with his arm extended, taking a blind swipe at whoever was there. His swing missed as the man stepped back. It wasn't the stranger he had seen on the road.

"You're not doing this tonight," said Soleil. He had also likely summoned his body to the car in the gravel lot.

Darren lowered the blade to his side, but his grip was tight. "I'll go through you if I have to," he said as he sized up Soleil, who was wearing his poncho. The outfit was different from the last time he had seen it. Several pouches now held darts. "Looks like you've upped your game."

Soleil absent-mindedly tapped his thumb against a dart near his left floating rib. "I was sick of having to deconstruct people's masks or clothes in order to poison them."

"So you've branched out to include injections. I guess we think alike on some things. It was nice seeing you again, but I really need to get back to work."

Soleil pulled a vial out of its pouch. "No, you don't."

Darren snorted. "What're those going to do? I'll just heal the way I heal from everything else."

"Don't be so sure. It's like you said: I've upped my game. I've mixed extracts and I've been experimenting on animals. I've got blends that'll attack your lungs, heart, and central nervous system simultaneously. Our healing abilities are impressive, and you might recover from it, but I guarantee you'll slow down."

Darren raised his saw blade to show he wasn't backing out. Suddenly his attention was torn away by a scream that cut across the field, followed by gunfire. Soleil and Darren ran toward the group. Someone was on the ground, curled up with his hands wrapped around his chest. The others were firing in the same general direction, but it did not appear that any of them had eyes on their target.

Soleil threw a vial of powder into the air. When it reached its peak, he deconstructed the glass and created a gust of wind that carried the plume of poison in the direction the people were shooting. The powder spread and began to fall, but Darren produced another breeze to keep the cloud from hitting the ground. Then he deconstructed the guns of Tymbir and his friends.

"They're all unarmed," shouted Darren. "You can come out now." A man appeared from behind a distant tree.

"You're working with the Old Ticker?" said Soleil as the newcomer approached.

"What did you call me?" asked the masked man.

"Sounds like you have a nickname," said Darren.

The Old Ticker raised one of his guns.

"Wait," Darren shouted. He turned to Soleil. "I know you don't agree with what we're doing, but look around. It's a two-on-one fight now. All their guns are destroyed. They can't help you."

He took a moment to watch Soleil cringe at the reality of the statement. Flarence would have been able to reconstruct the group's weapons because he knew the mechanics of firearms. All Soleil knew was what a gun looked like from the outside. Thanks to his incompetence, he was on his own.

"I told you I'd go through you if I have to," Darren repeated. "Leave now and let us finish the job."

"I'd do it," said the Old Ticker. "I almost killed you last time."

"Last time was different," said Soleil. "Last time we weren't out in the open." He flipped the back of his poncho over his head like a hood and the next thing Darren knew he was covered with white powder. He hadn't noticed Soleil controlling the wind, directing the cloud of poison back toward them. Whatever had been in the vial was now falling all around them.

Darren held his breath, but based on how quickly Soleil's poisons acted, he had a feeling it was too late. His skin itched as he brushed the powder off his arm. His hands trembled but his magically enhanced immune system fought the poison, and the shaking lasted only for a moment. The Old Ticker's clothes protected much of his skin, but the top of his head was exposed and the bandana was not airtight. He must have breathed some of the powder too because he fell, his guns abandoned as his body jerked. Tymbir and his friends reacted the same way.

Soleil went over to the Old Ticker as he convulsed. Darren threw his saw blade, but Soleil pivoted and it flew past him. Darren summoned it back along its original path, but Soleil was expecting it and ducked, avoiding the second hit as Darren caught the blade. Soleil grabbed the spellcasting revolvers, pointing one at Darren and the other at the Old Ticker. "You know I'm not here to fight you. My goal was to prevent you from killing Tymbir, but in this case, I'm giving the Old Ticker priority. I'm taking him somewhere I can force answers out of him. I'm also taking Tymbir. Kill the rest of his group if you want, but don't follow me."

"Sorry, Soleil. I have some questions for him too." He charged, and Soleil fired one of the guns. Darren took the hit and kept moving forward, swinging his saw in an arc but missing as Soleil sidestepped. Soleil noticed the gun hadn't done any harm and stared at it blankly. Darren checked his body for damage, and though he hadn't been burned or frozen, he could feel the energy the gun had transferred to him and realized it had been set to summon when Soleil pulled the trigger. "Maybe you should get accustomed to that weapon before using it," he taunted.

He threw the saw at Soleil as he charged again. Soleil dodged the blade but Darren rammed him with his shoulder and knocked him to the ground. Then he kicked Soleil's wrist, sending one of the guns skipping across the grass. Darren dove and grabbed it. He spun around and aimed at Soleil, who was on his feet aiming his gun at Darren. They fired together. For an instant Darren, felt the shot, and his face became severely burned, but he suppressed his screams as his spell took effect. The summoning energy was still resonating in Darren's body, and when the blast from his gun struck Soleil, it formed a connection. Because Darren was bigger, Soleil was swept off his feet and pulled toward him. When he was close, Darren hit him in the chin with an uppercut, then summoned the saw blade back to his body as Soleil fell.

Darren brought the blade down, aiming for the soft tissue of Soleil's neck but instead hit bone as Soleil raised an arm instinctively to block the blow. The blade dug deep but the barrel of his gun was now pointed at Darren.

Darren shifted his weight and forced Soleil's hand to the side, but Soleil never pulled the trigger. While Darren was focused on the gun, he had removed a fluid-filled vial from his poncho. Its temperature increased as he thrust it toward Darren's face. A cloud of steam formed in the vial, and the pressure popped the cork off. Darren backed away as he wiped the droplets from his face. He was still for a moment, expecting to be overcome with the urge to vomit or for welts to appear, but nothing happened. "When are you going to learn that your poisons don't work? I can heal from anything you shoot me up with."

Soleil swung the revolver like a club and broke Darren's nose. Then he followed with a jab to Darren's throat. Frustrated, Darren let out a growl as he swung the blade, which Soleil made no attempt to block or avoid. The blade cut deep into his face as he shoved Darren, who nearly lost his balance and stumbled back several feet, dropping his gun and saw blade. He began to feel light-headed, and the world started spinning as he lurched toward Soleil for another attack. His mouth felt dry, and he had trouble speaking. "What . . . hap-en-ing?"

"You're healing," said Soleil, "but the poison I gave you is a double threat. You break down poisons quickly, but one of the metabolic products of that vapor is carbon monoxide. If you had anticipated this, you could have weakened the bonding affinity between it and your hemoglobin, but that's probably not going to happen now. I imagine it's hard to focus while you're succumbing to chemical asphyxiation."

"Can't . . . kill . . . me," Darren sputtered. "I . . . can't . . . die."

"The hell you can't," said Soleil. Darren felt pressure on his neck. "Your cells are having trouble transporting oxygen, and now you're not taking in any air at all. If I keep this up, you will die." The pressure eased, and Darren fell. He was still dizzy, but he could feel himself breathing again. He was on his back, staring up at the sky, but had the sensation of falling. For the first time since becoming Enchanted, he felt afraid, and also embarrassed. After all the punishment he had taken at the hands of Tymbir's gang, he could not accept the possibility that he was about to be killed by Soleil's toxic tea.

"Take this!" The voice wasn't Soleil's and sounded distant. Darren couldn't turn his head to see who said it. Soleil's screams were cut short, and the voice came back. "That's right, you'd better run!" Darren couldn't process what was happening. He lay still, trying to focus on breathing, trying to keep his eyes open, but his vision was blurry. His view of the sky was obstructed as a figure hovered above him and slowly came into focus.

It was the Old Ticker. His clothes and hair were stained with the white powder, his eyes were bloodshot, and he was still twitching slightly, but he was back on his feet. He must have recovered the gun that Darren had dropped and fought off Soleil. Through the haze of his disorientation, a realization came to Darren: If the Old Ticker was back on his feet, then so was Tymbir. He tried to sit up but his body felt like jelly. The Old Ticker put a hand on Darren's shoulder to steady him. "Don't move. Just try to stay with me. I'll take care of these guys, and then I'll get us out of here."

Darren thought he heard screaming. He thought he heard people begging for their lives. It was all a blur, and he let the dizziness take him completely, closing his eyes and hoping he would be able to open them again.

SOLEIL

He wasn't sure if his eyes were closed or not. Even if they were open there was no way for light to enter the room. "Dad," he called into the darkness. A dull fluorescent light filled the room generated by orbs that lined the stone walls of the cave where Mohinaux lived. It was a small, circular room with no decoration other than boulders which were his idea of furniture. Soleil slumped against the boulder he had summoned his body to and let his head droop to his chest. His father came to his side and lifted his chin. "Amanitin derivative," Soleil mumbled. "My vial broke. Got it on my skin. Can't feel anything. Do I have a gun?"

Mohinaux looked at Soleil's hand. "You do. You have a gun. Soleil, why do you have a gun?" Soleil didn't have the strength to respond or keep his head up any longer. He let his body fall limp against the boulder.

He had no way of knowing how long he had been asleep. When his senses started coming back there was a throbbing pain in his stomach. His first thought was to curl into a ball and wrap his arms around himself, but he found he was already doing that. He was on his side, his cheek pressed against the hard floor, but there wasn't dirt on the ground like in Mohinaux's cave. Instead, the floor was covered in white tile. There was light but it was from an electric bulb instead of the fluorescent orbs he had seen before blacking out. He rolled to take in his surroundings, and realized that he was lying on the bathroom floor of his restaurant/house with his head next to the toilet.

When he moved, his stomach turned, and with a great effort he hauled himself up to the rim and vomited until he was sure there wasn't anything left in him, and then fell into a fit of dry heaves. He reached up to flush the toilet and didn't see a sleeve on his arm. He looked down and noticed all his clothes were gone. A blanket had been draped over him but it had fallen off while he was vomiting. He was about to readjust the blanket but another sick feeling overtook him and he struggled to turn around to sit on the toilet seat. He groaned and gritted his teeth as he emptied his bowels.

He went back and forth like that for a long time. The problems were expected considering what he had absorbed. The poison was similar to the Death Cap mushrooms which attacked the liver and led to symptoms such as renal failure. Soleil called the poison amanitin because the effects were comparable, but the poison wasn't exactly the same as the one produced by the mushroom. The Enchanted tree produced a plethora of poisons and toxins similar to substances found elsewhere, but their chemical structures were modified to make them deadlier and react more quickly. The poison would have killed a normal person in minutes, but in Soleil's case he would just be miserable for a few hours as the compound was metabolized.

Convinced that his body was drained of as much fluid as it could spare, Soleil wrapped the sheet around his shoulders and entered his bedroom where Kevin Tymbir was secured to his bed with a rope and had duct tape over his mouth. He thrashed on the bed, trying to break free, but the ropes were too tight and as he moved they dug into his skin. Soleil felt queasy and chose not to untie him, not in the mood for a confrontation in the event Tymbir was violent after being freed.

He made his way downstairs to get a glass of water. In the restaurant area, Mohinaux was pacing around the tables like they were a maze, Flarence was slumped in a chair, and Claire was at the stove scooping a pile of scrambled eggs onto four plates. Soleil noticed the Old Ticker's gun resting on the counter and sat next to it. Claire gave him a glass of water and a plate of scrambled eggs with bits of bacon incorporated into them and a side of toast. "You've been out for almost twelve hours. However bad you're feeling right now, you probably need to put something in your stomach and rehydrate. Also, would it have killed you to get dressed before coming down here?"

"I would have, but I felt a little uncomfortable doing so in a room where a madman is thrashing around on my bed," he said as Claire walked around the counter with two more plates of scrambled eggs. She placed one of the plates next to Flarence as she sat down next to him. Flarence didn't stir at the smell of the food and Claire didn't try to wake him up. "Who tied Tymbir to my bed, and what's Flarence doing?"

Mohinaux took a seat next to Soleil. "When you appeared in my cave, I assumed you had gotten into trouble with Darren and used my astral projection to find Tymbir. When I found him, the Old Ticker was slaughtering his group. I also noticed Darren was in worse shape than you, and summoned my body to the field with the intention of killing him, but the Old Ticker was too much for me." He looked embarrassed as he admitted defeat. "I wasn't able to win that fight, but I know how much keeping Tymbir alive means to you, so I grabbed him and summoned us back to your cafe. You couldn't control your bodily functions and were sweating like crazy, so I took off your dirty clothes and gave you the sheet. As for Flarence, he's projecting, either focusing on Stewart or Gil." Mohinaux took a bite of his eggs. "He became frustrated trying to figure out what was wrong with the gun and decided to focus on the Inspector R.E.D. problem."

Soleil was feeling a little better, but when he took a bite of his toast, it didn't settle in his stomach well. He picked up the gun. "What have you learned about it? Does it fire magic bullets?"

"That's one of the interesting things about the gun," said Mohinaux. "There aren't any bullets in it."

"What about in the barrel? Is there some kind of magic source in there?"

"You want to stick your eye up to the barrel and check? Be my guest," said Claire.

Mohinaux looked like he was going to say something but instead began shoveling eggs greedily into his mouth as if it was the most delicious meal he'd eaten in a long time. Considering that he lived in a cave and ate nothing but raw meat from animals he trapped, it probably was. Claire spoke up so he wouldn't have to talk with his mouth full. "Flarence took a look at the devices in the chambers. None of us have ever seen machines like them, but there doesn't appear to be anything supernatural about them. We're not sure exactly what the power source is, but all the wires look like they lead to the same place."

Soleil put down the gun, took another bite of his food and mentally begged it to stay down. "Have you tried looking into its past? Finding out where it was made and who designed it?"

"Flarence and I tried that," said Mohinaux, his plate scraped clean, "but it didn't work. I'm not sure how, but the gun itself seems to be Enchanted and resists spells." He produced a screwdriver from his pocket and slid the gun toward himself. "Flarence brought this from home and we poked around with it a little." Mohinaux placed the screwdriver against a bolt on the grip of the gun and turned it just enough for a section to lift a centimeter from its position. As it rose, Soleil felt a change in the room. The air became warmer, and also felt denser. The lights flickered, and some of the eggs on Soleil's plate became charred. Mohinaux turned the screwdriver in the opposite direction, bringing the pad back into its original position, and the room returned to normal.

"What was that?" said Soleil.

"We don't know. That's what frustrated Flarence so much," said Mohinaux. "It's also where the wires converge."

Soleil examined the weapon. Sure enough, there were three holes drilled in each side of the gun, with a wire connecting each hole to the energy source in the grip. Like Flarence's Stakehail Colt, the gun had no hammer to pull back. Instead, each wire looped through the empty spot where the hammer should have been and was fed into the cylinder. There was also a switch on the gun. Soleil pressed it and watched as the wires shifted outward and the cylinder spun clockwise. When he released the switch, the wires shifted again, repositioning into the selected chamber. He clicked the switch a few more times, watching the wires pivot and the cylinder turn. He released the cylinder and removed one of the gizmos inside. He closed his fingers around the device and tried looking into the machine's past. "I told you, we already tried that," came Mohinaux's voice, but it sounded distant since Soleil was already gone.

Just as in the morgue, the vision came to Soleil like a dream. Unlike at the morgue, though, the experience was disorienting. Everything around him was hazy, as if he was walking through a thick fog, and even though he was standing on solid ground in his vision, he felt a tight pinch in the pit of his stomach like he was in freefall. The sensation made it impossible to maintain his focus, and he slipped out of the vision, returning to his cafe and falling out of his chair. Mohinaux was by his side, taking one of his arms to help him up. The blanket slipped off his shoulders, exposing his chest, but he was able to hold onto it before it fell below his waist. When he was seated again, Soleil took a sip of water and removed another of the devices from the cylinder.

"I'm glad you're taking this so seriously," said Claire, "but before you do anything else, please put some clothes on." Soleil ignored her. He clenched the machine in his fist tightly and took a few deep breaths, preparing for another try.

"It won't work, Soleil," said Mohinaux. "Flarence and I have already tried the psychometry spell on the different parts of the gun. They all resist our efforts."

"I don't care," said Soleil. "I got poisoned getting my hands on it." He closed his eyes and forced the vision to return. He was going to get something useful. Anything. This attempt wasn't any easier than the last one, and the same feeling of vertigo overtook him as the world was lost in a haze. This wasn't supposed to be happening. None of this was supposed to be happening. Objects couldn't be Enchanted. People couldn't be brought back from the dead. Spells couldn't affect Genies. It was as if the universe suddenly decided to abolish everything he'd ever learned.

Soleil fought hard to hold onto his vision. In his mind, he fell to one knee and stared at the ground, waiting for the feeling of weightlessness to pass, but it just became worse. The ground around his feet was changing. One moment it was coated with frost, the next it was soaking wet, and then it was baking in the sun. It was as if the seasons were making random jumps between summer and winter. One thing that stayed the same was the lack of grass. Holding on to something that stayed constant eased the nausea. I'm on pavement, he thought; that's a start. He pushed himself up and took a step forward, struggling to maintain his balance. He looked up and noticed that the sky was changing as fast as the pavement, going from day to night, cloudy to clear, in the blink of an eye. He brought his head down and tried to take in his surroundings, looking for anything that was staying consistent.

A car appeared in front of him, and he had just enough time to notice the hood ornament before it was gone. Soleil stared at the spot where the vehicle had been, and a few seconds later, another car, smaller and unfamiliar, took its place. Soleil wasn't an expert on cars but knew the logos of all the major companies, and this one was completely alien to him. Soon, the unknown car disappeared, but there was a pattern. Two cars had appeared in a row, and he was standing on pavement. He concluded that he was in a parking lot, and the nausea faded a little more. He saw movement in his peripheral vision, but by the time he turned his head, whatever had been there was gone.

If he was in a parking lot, there must be a building nearby, which was probably where the machine had been developed. People walked by him, and, like the cars, disappeared quickly, but Soleil had seen their direction and followed their path. A few uneven steps through the mist of changing weather brought him to a glass door where he was greeted with another unfamiliar logo accompanied by the words S&D Technologies. Beneath the company name, the address was stenciled on the glass: 1840 Hudson Avenue. He released his hold and fell out of the vision. He was having a hard time opening his eyes, and could feel the cold floor on his exposed skin.

"Are you back?" It was Mohinaux's voice.

"Are you all right?" Claire this time.

"I fell off the chair again, didn't I?" Soleil asked as he forced his eyes open.

"You were shaking and blurting out a bunch of nonsense," said Mohinaux as he stood Soleil up and brought him back to the counter, this time more careful to keep the blanket from slipping off.

"It was worth it," said Soleil as he picked at his eggs and sipped his water. "I saw the building where the device was developed. I got its address."

"We know," said Claire, "it's one of the things you blurted out. You also said something about sandy technology."

"S&D Technology," said Soleil. "That's the name of the company. The Old Ticker might not work there, but it's at least a lead on where part of his gun was made. Is Flarence conscious yet? We should fill him in." The three of them turned to where Flarence had been sitting a moment ago, but he was gone. The eggs had not been touched, and the chair was not pushed back under the table.

"To answer your question, yes, Flarence is conscious," said Mohinaux.

"He's gone?" said Soleil. "What kind of guy sneaks out of a room while his brother is having a seizure?"

"Don't take it personally," said Claire. "I'm sure he'll be back soon. He must have noticed something important regarding Inspector R.E.D."

Soleil took another bite of his eggs. "Dad, we should go look for the S&D Technology building. We'll take Tymbir and the gun with us. It doesn't feel right leaving him tied up like that. Darren could come for him. Claire, when Flarence gets back, fill him in on what we learned." As he walked toward the table to move Flarence's chair, his foot stepped on part of the blanket and caused it to slip again. He barely managed to catch it before it fell around his feet.

"What part of put some clothes on don't you understand?" said Claire.

Soleil sheepishly readjusted the blanket as he climbed the steps to his room.

FLARENCE

The poor woman was understandably terrified, unaware that she was fighting the man who was trying to save her. When Flarence appeared in her house, his plan was to grab her and summon them both somewhere safe, but she had better reflexes than he'd anticipated.

He didn't have time to tell anyone where he was going. He had been performing an astral projection in Soleil's Cafe and was going back and forth between following Stewart and Gil. Neither had been attacked and things at the factory were running smoothly, which bothered Flarence. Was Roy waiting for something? Was he planning something especially cruel for the two brothers?

While projecting, Flarence overheard Stewart making a call to a woman named Emma, whom he deduced was his wife based on the conversation. He had also discovered that Emma was several months pregnant. He didn't know how long they'd been married, but he had a feeling that she was in danger. There was no way Stewart would forgive Gil if Roy killed Emma and the unborn child. Flarence projected to Stewart's house and found Emma home alone putting handfuls of fruit and ice in a blender. Roy was crouched behind a bush outside, watching her through a kitchen window.

Fearing what Roy had planned, Flarence's projection returned to his body, and as soon as he was conscious, he attached his Wrist Cannon to his right arm and summoned his body to the refrigerator in Emma's kitchen. Unfortunately, she was facing the refrigerator, and when he appeared, she panicked. She unplugged the blender and threw it at Flarence, soaking him in fruit juice. Then she advanced on him with the knife she been using to cut the fruit. It wasn't the entrance he had planned, but she moved away from the window just before Roy came crashing through it. Flarence drew his Stakehail Colt and flipped the switch to open it, but Roy ran while he was loading and was gone by the time the icicles and carbon dioxide were ready.

Emma took a step toward Flarence, who put his hands up, attempting to look peaceful. "You're pointing that knife at the wrong guy. I know Stewart. My name's Flarence and I'm here to help."

"Help with what? What was that thing?" said Emma.

"That's Inspector R.E.D.," said Flarence. "Apparently, he's back from the dead. I can get you out of here if you take my hand." Emma didn't move. "You can keep the knife if it makes you feel more comfortable, but you really need to take my hand."

Emma extended one hand, but with the other, she kept the blade pointed at Flarence. "I'm keeping the knife."

Before their hands could touch, though, there was a crash, and Roy was standing between them. He had gone to the upper level of the house, stood above them, and then pounded his way through the floor with a single stomp. Flarence didn't have time to react, and Roy delivered a punch that made him see stars. Before he could shake off the dizziness, Roy had his hands on his collar and threw him across the room.

"So Stewart hired some backup, did he?" said Roy as he approached Flarence with his fists clenched. Flarence fired at Roy's neck. Roy bobbed and the icicle whizzed over his head. Flarence fired again and Roy dodged it as easily as the first one. He fired the last four rounds in rapid succession. Roy dodged three of them and caught the fourth. He lunged and stabbed Flarence in the stomach with it. "You can't hurt me," he said as he broke Flarence's wrist to make him drop the gun. A punch to the temple sent Flarence sprawling on the floor.

Flarence shook away the blurriness as his wrist popped back into place. Roy turned to Emma, and while his back was turned, Flarence pulled the icicle out of his stomach and drove it into the back of Roy's leg. When he was down, Flarence delivered a right hook with the Wrist Cannon, sending the brass knob smashing into Roy's skull. "Neither can you," he said as Roy fell forward. He stood up and kicked Roy in the ribs. Roy flipped onto his back and the bullets sprang from his chest. The metal shards stayed suspended in the air for a moment before flying to Flarence, sinking deep into his body.

Flarence tried to push through the pain. He prepared to hit Roy in the face with the Wrist Cannon but fell over before he could land the blow. He felt the metal moving inside him as Roy controlled the bullets, forcing them throughout Flarence's body and making them tear through his organs. Flarence tried to summon the bullets to something in the kitchen, or back to Roy, but the pain was too intense for him to concentrate. He just rolled on the floor clutching his chest and stomach as the metal shards shredded his innards. His body stitched itself back together but was unable to keep up with the damage the bullets were doing. Just when he thought he was going to pass out, the bullets exited his body at random points and returned to Roy's chest.

The pain wasn't accumulating anymore, but Flarence still felt his whole body throbbing. He lifted his shirt and saw that most of his torso was covered with dark splotches from all the places he was bleeding internally. As the bruises shrank and the pain subsided, he rose to his hands and knees and looked around, seeing what had made Roy call the bullets back to his body.

Emma was holding the knife and thrusting it at Roy, backing him into a corner. If she was freaked out, she was hiding it well. She wasn't screaming like a maniac or swinging the knife wildly, but instead kept the blade still and poised to strike quickly. Her face was angry but not flustered. Her strikes were quick and calculated, as if she had experience with weapons. Emma thrust at his face and cut part of the stupid mask he wore. Roy didn't bring his hand up to the cut, and Flarence wondered if he even felt pain. Blood didn't flow from the wound the way it would on a normal person. Instead, it oozed out as thick pus, staining the mask and clotting to form a crust that stopped the flow. Emma stopped attacking. Her face changed from one of anger to one of fright, and she backed away. For every step she took backward, Roy stepped forward.

Now Emma started freaking out. Instead of making quick, precise strikes with the knife, she was making more of a sweeping motion with her arms, lashing out with swings that were wide and easy for Roy to avoid. With his incredible speed, he wrenched the blade from Emma's hand, bent it in half easily, and tossed it across the room. Emma backed away and frantically looked around. Her eyes fell on Flarence's gun. She ran to it, picked it up, and pointed it at Roy. The moment she pulled the trigger, Roy bolted from the room as if on instinct, but it was pointless since the gun was not loaded. Emma continued pulling the trigger, aiming where Roy had been a moment ago, frustrated that nothing was happening. "How do you work this thing?" she shouted.

"Like this," said Flarence. He stood up, took the gun from her, and reloaded it. He caught movement in his peripheral vision and without taking the time to aim fired in the direction he thought Roy was coming from. The shot was wild but close enough to make Roy run out of the room again. A moment later, there was a creak above them, and Roy jumped into the kitchen from the hole in the ceiling he had made earlier. Flarence fired, and this time struck Roy in the chest. Roy pulled the icicle from his body. As with Emma's cut, he did not scream in pain, and the wound crusted shut rather than bleed profusely. Deciding to retreat, Flarence turned to Emma, who was still in a state of panic but was thankfully within reaching distance. He hugged Emma and summoned his body back to Soleil's Cafe.

They arrived safely by the counter. Emma's face was flushed and she spun around the room, taking in the new scenery, looking like she wanted to shout but not knowing what to say. Flarence realized the water was running and turned to find Claire standing at the sink scrubbing dishes. She dropped a plate in the soapy water as she gaped at the pregnant and frightened woman and then at Flarence, who had both his weapons out, his shirt untucked and stained with fruit juice. "Believe it or not," he said, "I can explain."

—4—

DARREN

He had no idea where he was, but was aware that he had been lying on a smelly mattress for a while. Every time he woke he would try to get up and walk around, only to be overcome with lightheadedness, fall back down, and drift to unconsciousness again. His memory from the fight was hazy, but Soleil had clearly done a number on him. Finally, he could stay awake long enough to take in his surroundings. He was in a cold, cramped space with multiple blankets covering his body. There was no natural light, and a strong draft brought a chill as well as an overpowering smell of car exhaust and urine. At first, he thought he was in a room with very poor ventilation but then realized he wasn't in a room at all. The roof above him was dark brown, stained with water damage, and had creases in it. He realized that his shelter was a cardboard box with one of its sides cut out so it could surround his bed, which he now noticed was a sleeping bag instead of a mattress. In addition to the sound of the wind, there was an ear-splitting noise that was giving him a headache.

He rolled out of the sleeping bag and crawled out of the box. The light was dim because he was surrounded by concrete. He also noticed that he had been sleeping next to an intersection, and the noise that had been giving him a headache came from cars rushing by. Someone tried to turn who shouldn't have, and another driver honked, which made Darren feel like his head was going to explode. "It's about time you woke up," said a voice behind him. Darren spun around to see a man standing by a shopping cart with his hands in the pockets of a brown hoodie. When the man, pulled the hood down to reveal his face, Darren guessed that he was in his late 40s or early 50s. His hair was short and mostly black but stained with gray streaks. There were wiry patches of facial hair on his chin and neck, and the remnants of a five o'clock shadow. He wore black denim jeans and a pair of heavy-duty work boots. As Darren approached, the man reached into the shopping cart and took out a box of grapes.

"It's not much," he said, "but it's all I could swipe from the farmer's market." Darren was hungry but didn't accept the food right away. The two of them stood there, studying each other. The man had the same eyes and hair as the gunman Darren had encountered before, but without the mask, he couldn't be sure it was the same person. The man pulled a piece of fabric from a pocket. He held it out for only a moment, but it was long enough for Darren to see the image of a clock on it.

"It's me. I saved you in the field, and I've been keeping you warm while you recovered. You've been out almost a full day." Darren took the box and popped a small fruit into his mouth. The man put a ceramic plate in the middle of the shopping cart and lined it with strips of raw bacon. "This is something else I swiped," he said as he unzipped his hoodie and pulled out a revolver which he pointed at the food. He squeezed the trigger and the bacon sizzled. He flipped the strips over and cooked the other side, then put the gun back in his shoulder holster and zipped the hoodie.

"Right now, we're under Wacker Drive," said the man as he and Darren helped themselves to the bacon. "It'll be much easier to move around now that you're awake. My name's Wicker, Doctor Emanuel Wicker. My friends call me Manny, although I guess you can call me the Old Ticker now."

"I'm Darren Raleigh."

"Nice to meet you. If you want me to explain how my guns work, we should find someplace quiet where we can sit down."

Dr. Wicker moved to the cardboard box and started rolling up the sleeping bag, but Darren stopped him. "You can explain the gun later. I'm more interested in Tymbir. Did you kill him?"

"No, and I don't plan on it," said Dr. Wicker as he produced a folded piece of paper and handed it to Darren. Names were written on every line. Darren scanned the paper looking for Tymbir, Soleil, Flarence, Claire, or Mohinaux. None of their names were written down, but among the crossed off ones were some people Darren used to know.

"You killed a bunch of my friends that day I saw you in the apartment."

"I'm sorry that you knew some of the people, but everything I've done was part of a greater purpose. Trust me, all this is leading to something big. Unfortunately, I hit a bump in the road last night. I fought off the nutcase with the vials sewn to his poncho, but he took one of my guns. Then another person appeared out of nowhere. I fought him off as well, but not before he grabbed a guy and the two of them just disappeared. I took the driver's licenses from the people I killed to confirm their identity. Tymbir wasn't one of them."

Darren picked up another strip of bacon. "Did you kill anyone else? Students? Teachers?"

"No," said Dr. Wicker. "Students and teachers don't fit the descriptions." He went to the pillow near the sleeping bag, reached in, and pulled out a leather pouch. Then he opened the flap and removed a stack of papers. Darren selected one at random. On one side was a man's face, and on the other the name Corey Willard was written, followed by a bullet-pointed list of characteristics such as height, weight, marital status, where he lived, and where he worked. "I've done a background check on each of my targets," explained Dr. Wicker. "Nobody on my list works at a university, or is named Tymbir."

Darren gave the list back to Dr. Wicker. "The man you saw last night with the vials is Soleil. He has friends, and they're probably all working together to protect Tymbir now."

"No problem. I'll help you get to him if you help me take care of the rest of my list. I happen to know some of the people live nearby."

Darren took several more grapes and backed away from Dr. Wicker. "You can't expect me to trust you," he said.

"I can't make up for what happened before," said Dr. Wicker. "Quite a few of my targets were located in that apartment. I didn't know some of them were your friends. I didn't even know about you. I still don't know what you are or how you do what you do, but I believe we can help each other. It's why I saved you in that field."

"Look," said Darren, "I appreciate you helping me and for keeping an eye on me and for the bacon and the grapes, but you don't understand what I'm doing. I'm not some lunatic killing people at random. Tymbir ruined my life, and I want to make him suffer for it. The rest of the names on your list are your problem." Darren turned and walked away. If the Old Ticker was telling the truth, he was in the home stretch. Tymbir was separated from his friends now. It was time to finish the job.

SOLEIL

"Another dead end," said Soleil. He was standing with Mohinaux and Tymbir at 1840 Hudson Avenue, but it was nothing like what Soleil had seen with his psychometry spell. The address in Chicago was a fast food restaurant. Soleil was sure he had seen the address right in the vision, but he realized that nothing indicated it was in Chicago, or even in Illinois at all. Tymbir had been reluctant to go with them but proved useful in searching for the address and pulling maps up on his phone. He also tried typing S&D Technology into a search engine, but the results didn't seem like the kind of companies that would manufacture the machines that were in the gun, or were located at the right address. They were walking down Hudson Avenue in Tulsa, where they were greeted by a simple brick house. "Let's get moving. Tymbir, where's the next one?"

"No way," said Tymbir. "So far we've been taking shot after shot in the dark. Maybe that works for you two, but I used to be a cop. I'm more coordinated than that."

"We don't have a lot to go on," said Soleil. "I couldn't find a ton of information from my vision."

"Then let me see the gun," said Tymbir. "I can track down the person who bought it."

"We're not giving you the gun," said Soleil. "Besides, you're not a cop anymore."

"I know a guy who can help us out," said Tymbir. "We were friends and worked together. As far as I know, he's still employed."

"Give me his name and I'll pay him a visit," said Mohinaux. "I just need to get my shirt."

"You won't need to force him to help us," said Tymbir. "Like I said, we were friends. We haven't seen each other for a while, but he'll help if I ask. Just give me the gun and do that quick travel thing you do."

"It's called a summoning spell," said Mohinaux, "and that's not going to happen."

"I don't like the situation any more than you do" said Tymbir, "but if we're going to work together, then we need to trust each other."

"I trust you know what you're doing," said Soleil, "so tell us where your friend lives and we'll go there together, but you're not touching the gun under any circumstances."

Tymbir told them where his friend lived, and Mohinaux supported Soleil who sent his astral projection to the house. "Nobody's home," he said as his projection returned to his body.

"Of course he's not home," said Tymbir. "It's the middle of the day, and he still has a job."

"We'll try the house again in a few hours," said Mohinaux. "In the meantime, we should keep searching. Find another Hudson Avenue."

The three of them spent hours traveling to every Hudson Avenue, Street, and Drive that Tymbir's phone could find. When Soleil sent his astral projection again to the house they had tried, he found a man in the kitchen preparing spaghetti with canned red sauce.

Soleil's projection returned to his body, and the three of them went there together.

When the man answered the door, he didn't move at first. He took a deep breath, preparing to say something, and then cringed.

"I know," said Tymbir. "I smell terrible. Can we come in?" The three of them moved past the man into the kitchen. "Sit down, Jason," said Tymbir.

The water reached a boil as the three took seats at the kitchen table. "It's been a while," said Tymbir. "Guys, this is Jason. We go way back. He was the one person in the police department I talked to when I was trying to kill Darren."

"I thought you were having a nervous breakdown," said Jason. "Before you disappeared, you told me about a magical gangster."

"And now I'm going to tell you about a magical gun," said Tymbir.

Soleil held the spellcasting revolver up for Jason to see. "We don't know how it works or who made it. Tymbir said you might be able to track down the owner." He tilted the gun so Jason could see the digits imprinted on the metal.

Jason leaned forward to get a closer look, then sat back down. "I can look into the gun, but I can already tell you the number's been altered."

"You can tell just by glancing at it?" said Soleil.

"Most people scratch out serial numbers when they don't want their guns tracked," said Jason, "but it looks like the owner of this one added digits. No gun has a serial number that long. Tymbir should have been able to tell you that much."

"See, this is why you should trust me," said Tymbir. "I could have saved us all a trip and a few hours."

"We're leaving," said Mohinaux. "Don't try to follow us."

"Wait," said Jason as Soleil went to the door, "what did you mean when you said the gun was magic?"

"That's none of your concern," said Mohinaux. "Like I said, don't try to follow us. Also, don't tell anyone we were here. Finish cooking your dinner as if nothing happened." Mohinaux grabbed Tymbir by the collar and hauled him out of the house. Soleil followed, and when they reached a safe spot, they summoned their bodies to the cafe.

"Well, that got us nowhere," said Soleil as he went to the refrigerator and took a bottle of soda. When he turned around, Flarence and Claire were sitting at a table, with a man and a woman sitting across from them arm-in-arm.

FLARENCE

Tymbir went to take a seat at the counter. "Not there," said Mohinaux. He grabbed Tymbir's elbow and moved some tables around until there was a chair sitting in a vacant spot like an island. "If you don't want to sit near us, that's fine, but Darren can summon his body to that counter and cut your throat before we even know he's there. From now on, whenever you go anywhere, you need to stay away from large objects, and when you're in a room, stay away from the walls."

Mohinaux and Soleil each took a chair to the table where Flarence and Claire were sitting. Flarence gestured to the couple. "Stewart, Emma, this is my Dad and my brother. Dad, Soleil, these are some of the people Inspector R.E.D.'s been targeting."

"I'm glad you're making progress," said Soleil. "We pretty much wasted the entire day trying to track down the building I saw in my vision."

"I don't think it was a waste," said Mohinaux as he turned to Flarence. "We took the gun to Tymbir's friend who thought the owner added digits to the serial number, but I think it might be legitimate." He put the gun on the table and stared at it like he was deeply focused, but nothing happened. Then he released the cylinder and took out one of the small devices. He held his hand flat, resting it in the center of his palm, and scooted several feet away from the table and the rest of the gun. He made the device levitate and kept it suspended for a moment before letting it fall back down and returning to the table. "Whatever is in the grip of the gun resists magical influence and prevents our spells from taking effect when it's all put together. But the components of gun don't resist all spells. It's just the psychometry spell that doesn't work. I think the reason we can't look into its past is because it doesn't have one. Or, more accurately, I think we're looking into a past that hasn't happened yet."

The nice thing about being in a family of Genies was that everyone had an open mind. "I did think those small machines in the gun were strange," said Soleil as he considered what Mohinaux said. "It almost seems like the gun is made from technology that doesn't exist. So you think we're dealing with a spell-shooting assassin from the future."

"Wait a minute," said Claire. "If the Old Ticker is from the future, can you guys cast time travel spells?"

"I don't think so," said Flarence, "but I've never tried." He stood up, closed his eyes and focused on transporting his body an hour into the past. When he opened them, he was still standing in front of the table. Claire shook her head, indicating that nothing had happened. Flarence closed his eyes again and tried traveling only a minute back in time, but when he opened his eyes, Claire shook her head again.

Flarence cracked his neck and prepared for a third attempt, but Mohinaux interrupted him. "Even if it were in our power, we'd need to know the principles of time distortion before we could cast a spell. I needed to study electricity before discovering how to use my powers to influence it." Flarence looked at Claire, shrugged, and sat back down.

"Where do we stand on the Inspector R.E.D. issue?" asked Soleil.

"Like you and Dad, I don't know anything for sure," said Flarence. "I've met him, and based on the way he fights, I don't think he can use magic the way we can. The bullets in his chest hovered above his body before smashing into me, but that was it. He didn't mentally break my gun, and instead of deconstructing the walls of the room, he just crashed right through them."

"We're still not sure how Darren did it," said Claire, "but based on what we've learned so far, it seems like Inspector R.E.D.'s powers are strictly internal. He can magically enhance his physical abilities and become as fast or strong as he wants. I guess the metal shards in his chest are a part of him now, which is why he can control them, but that seems to be the extent of his ability to influence objects."

"There's something else," said Flarence. "It seems he doesn't feel pain. I hit him really hard when I was at Emma's house, but it didn't seem to bother him. Also, Emma cut his face and the wound didn't heal, but the blood clotted really fast."

"Maybe the blood is magic," said Soleil. He rubbed his temples as his eyes narrowed. "Maybe his blood isn't his. When I caught up with Darren the other night, he noticed that I added darts to my toxic poncho and commented on the inclusion of injections. He said we think alike. I didn't dwell on it at the time, but what if it had something to do with how he revived Inspector R.E.D? What if Darren injected a corpse with his blood, and the result was reanimation?"

"Have you ever done that?" Flarence asked Mohinaux.

"No," said Mohinaux. "I've Enchanted a lot of animals but never by sharing my blood."

"If that really is how he did it, then the problem might solve itself," said Soleil. "In spite of all our power, Genies are the same as normal people where it counts. Our cells break down and new ones are formed. If Inspector R.E.D. really was reanimated by Darren's blood, then he's running on fumes. The blood cells will eventually break down."

"Possibly," said Mohinaux, "but we can't rely on that. A typical person's life span is less than a hundred years, but I've been alive for thousands. An ordinary person's blood cells break down in only a matter of months, but Enchanted cells could last decades. Even if his Enchanted cells aren't being naturally replaced, Inspector R.E.D. probably isn't going away any time soon."

Claire turned to Stewart and Emma, who had been sitting quietly, their eyes darting from speaker to speaker. "Are you getting this? Inspector R.E.D. is coming for you, and stopping him is going to be tough. In order to get the drop on him, we need to anticipate his next move. We know why he's going after Stewart and Gil, but why did he come to you today?"

"He didn't crash into the kitchen until Flarence showed up," said Emma. "He might have seen a guy in a suit and thought it was Stu. I don't think he wanted to hurt me. When Inspector—I mean, when Roy—started investigating Stu and Gil's factory, we actually spent a lot of time together. He was a good guy. We were friends. Stu and I even had him over for dinner a few times. The moment he thought something illegal was going on at the factory, he came to me. He didn't care what happened to Gil, but he knew Stu and I had been planning on starting a family and didn't want any legal trouble to get in the way of that."

"If you and Inspector R.E.D. were friends when he was alive, then we might be able to convince him not to kill you," said Flarence. "Gil, though, is a probably a goner. He's the one who pulled the trigger, so it's safe to assume Roy really hates his guts. We better start keeping a closer eye on him."

"He should be safe where he is, or at least difficult to find," said Stewart. "He's staying at a friend's house. Well, she's not really a friend. She's one of many women Gil made promises to. He told her that our business would be booming someday which would make him filthy rich. If he doesn't come through on that promise soon, their relationship is going to go downhill fast."

Flarence performed an astral projection to observe the farmhouse. It wasn't long before his limp body shot up like he'd had a nightmare. "Gil isn't safe," he said. "Inspector R.E.D. tracked him down. He's outside the house right now. He's planning something."

Soleil summoned his toxic poncho from his room, and Mohinaux vanished, returning a moment later wearing his shirt with his collar, sunglasses, and hat covering most of his face. Claire donned her Razor Punk attire while Flarence slipped on his Wrist Cannon. Soleil held Stewart and Emma, Mohinaux held Tymbir, and

Flarence held Claire. The cafe was vacant as each of the Genies performed a summoning spell targeting a bookcase in the woman's living room.

$$-5-$$

DARREN

As he figured, Tymbir was the one who had been saved that night in the field, and he was under constant surveillance. After leaving Dr. Wicker in the street, Darren had gone to the nearest train station. Keeping up his cover as a homeless man, he sat cross-legged against a pillar with a Styrofoam cup in front of him, as well as a section of a discarded pizza box that he'd scribbled a message on asking passersby for any money they could spare.

While resting against the pillar, he had been periodically sending his astral projection to Tymbir, looking for an opportunity to finish the job. Unfortunately, Soleil and Mohinaux were always nearby, and Darren was getting frustrated. The thought occurred to him that it might not matter if Soleil and Mohinaux were providing protection. One lucky shot with his saw blade and Tymbir would be history. Darren decided he was going to slash the man's throat, with or without Soleil and Mohinaux watching.

His last astral projection had seen Tymbir sitting in the middle of Soleil's Cafe while everyone else was at a table talking with two people Darren didn't recognize. It wasn't the ideal situation, but the Genies were distracted. The moment nobody else was on the platform, Darren removed his saw blade and summoned his body to the counter.

He tore through the cafe to the chair where his projection had seen Tymbir, nearly reaching it before realizing the room was empty. He checked the dining area and Soleil's room, which were also deserted. He performed another astral projection, locating Tymbir in an unknown house. But this time he had no opening at all. Tymbir was standing between Soleil and Mohinaux while Flarence was having a heated discussion with another man in the room. If he was going to kill Tymbir, the surprise entry wasn't going to work. His projection floated through the ceiling and observed the area. The house was small and secluded, with a barn nearby and acres of what may once have been corn. But it was late in the year and the crops had been harvested. Walking through the snow, sticking out in his dark clothes, was Dr. Wicker.

Darren summoned his body to an outer wall of the house below a kitchen window. Inside he could hear Flarence and another man shouting, but they were talking too loud and fast for him to make sense of what they were saying. He manipulated gravity as he kicked off from the wall and glided across the field like a phantom.

"Tymbir's mine," said Darren as he landed in front of Dr. Wicker.

"Actually, I'm here for someone named Amanda Raik. Her name's on my list."

"I don't know who that is, but Tymbir is in there, along with Soleil and his friends. You've seen what Soleil's capable of on his own, and he's the soft one. You can't take them all on by yourself."

"It sounds like we're going to have to work together. Let's see if we can find a way to get in unnoticed." Dr. Wicker's gaze drifted away from the house. "It looks like we might be getting some practice before we go in." He gestured behind Darren, who turned and saw someone leaving the barn wearing a white lab coat stained with red splotches and carrying a long blade that seemed to have been wrenched off a machine in the barn. He walked with a hunch, and there was no cloud surrounding his mask, even though his breath should have been visible in the cold. Dr. Wicker spun the cylinder on his gun and raised it. "I think I can take him out from here with a shock."

"Wait," said Darren, catching Dr. Wicker's wrist. "The way he's walking and the fact that he doesn't seem to be breathing. . . . I think I know that guy."

SOLEIL

Gil was inches in front of Flarence's face. "I'm done talking. If he tracked me here, then we need to leave right now." Flarence shook his head, and Gil punched him in the jaw, which Flarence took without flinching. Gil ran for the front door, but Soleil was standing in front of it.

"It's time to make a stand," said Soleil as he pushed Gil away. "Too much has happened that we can't comprehend. Tonight, we eliminate a threat. When Inspector R.E.D. comes for you, we'll be ready for him."

"What if you're not?" said Gil.

"Then it's a good thing you're the bait," said Flarence. "From what I hear, you're the killer. If something bad happens, you had it coming."

The woman who owned the house—Amanda, Soleil had learned—ran to Gil and wrapped her arms around him. "This is crazy! You can't use my man as bait. He's a good person. Please, whatever's going on here, just leave us out of it."

"Look, you don't have to do anything," said Claire. "Just run and hide somewhere when he shows up. We'll take care of all the dirty work."

"Emma, this is Roy we're talking about," said Gil. "You can't possibly be okay with this."

"Roy's become a monster," said Emma. "If there's any of the old him left, I hope we can bring it back, but he's a completely different person. After seeing what he's capable of, I can say without a doubt there's no prison that can hold him. If we can't reason with him, then he needs to be put down. Is there a gun in the house?"

"You're all insane," said Amanda. "I want you all out." She went to the door and tried to push Soleil away, but he increased his weight and didn't budge. Amanda took a step back and drove her shoulder into him, but it was like trying to tip over a tree. Finally, she gave up and stood in front of him with her hands on her hips. "I told you we're done here. This is my house. I'm in charge here, and I told you to get. . . ."

There was a crunching sound as a long, sharp piece of metal penetrated the door. It traveled straight through Soleil before going into Amanda. Soleil backed away from the door as Roy tore it off its hinges. He tried to take a vial from his poncho but wasn't quick enough, and Roy delivered a punch to the temple which knocked him down. "Bleed as I bled, you fucking shithead!" The bullets burst from his chest and flew toward Gil.

Flarence ran into the path of the bullets. Mohinaux lunged at Roy, pinning him against a wall with one hand and punching him in the face with the other. He landed three hits before the bullets flew out of Flarence back into Roy. As they painfully tore through his body, the metal shards made Mohinaux lose his grip, and Roy threw him across the room.

Gil had taken Claire's advice and run for a place to hide. Flarence and Claire kept Roy busy as Mohinaux knelt over Amanda and held a glove over her wound to stop the bleeding. Tymbir, Emma, and Stewart stood together in a corner. Soleil looked at Amanda's wound. The cut was deep but he hoped his body had slowed the blade enough to keep the injury from threatening Amanda's life. He lifted her shirt and applied a potent clotting agent that slowed the blood flow, but she was still breathing fast, and when Soleil improved his senses, he could hear her heart racing.

Suddenly there was a crash that sounded like a bomb to him. He turned to see a hole in the wall. Flarence was no longer in the room. Claire had a razor blade in each hand. She struck quickly, but Roy was faster. He ran around her, knocked Tymbir out of the way, and pinned Stewart against a wall. Flarence leaped through the hole in the wall and aimed the Stakehail Colt at Roy.

"You know I'm faster than that gun," said Roy. "If you shoot, I'll move out of the way and you'll hit Stewart."

"Roy, please stop," Emma begged. "We're going to be parents."

"That's even more reason to kill him," said Roy. "You don't want a murderer raising your child."

"It wasn't me," said Stewart. "I didn't even know Gil brought a gun that night. I had no idea what he was planning."

"But you knew he was capable of it," said Roy. "You didn't try to stop him when he pulled out his gun. Marcus, Evelyn, Adam—any one of you might as well have pulled the trigger."

"Roy, I'm so sorry," said Stewart, his eyes glistening with tears. "I want to make it up to you. I'll do anything you say. Please, tell me what you want. Anything at all."

"Begging isn't going to help," said Roy as he leaned in closer to Stewart. "You've got me seeing red. Now bleed as I bled." The bullets erupted from his chest.

"No!" shouted Emma.

"Stewart!" shouted Claire.

"What is it with you and rhymes?" said Flarence.

Roy dropped Stewart and stepped away as Emma ran to his limp body.

Soleil took a vial from his poncho and was about to throw it at Roy but turned when Amanda screamed. The Old Ticker stood in the doorway with one of his guns aimed at her. Soleil threw the vial at him instead. The Old Ticker flinched as Soleil deconstructed the vial, but the powder burst into flames and the ashes fluttered uselessly in the breeze as Darren also appeared. The Old Ticker fired a spell that hit Amanda's foot. Her shoe dissolved, as did the skin and muscle under it. She screamed and pulled her foot away before the spell could reach her bones. Soleil lifted her and carried her through the hole in the wall. The Old Ticker followed as Darren fixed his eyes on Tymbir.

FLARENCE

Roy ran up the stairs to the second floor where Gil had gone earlier. Darren threw the saw blade at Tymbir, but Claire dove in front, and the blade bounced off her chains. Flarence deconstructed the wall near where Stewart had been killed. "Emma, Tymbir, get out of here!" Neither of them needed to be told twice. They ran to the field with Claire following close, trying to keep them safe as Darren pursued Tymbir.

Flarence leaped through the ceiling into a bedroom and improved his senses. In the distance, he heard Roy overturning furniture as he looked for Gil. He also heard a heartbeat not far from where he was standing. He looked under the bed and saw Gil lying prone with a shotgun, ready to blow someone's leg off. Flarence pointed to the floor, mouthed the words "stay down," and stood up as Roy entered the room.

Flarence fired the Stakehail Colt. Roy ducked and the icicle became embedded in a wall. Flarence ran at him and tried to hit him with the Wrist Cannon. But Roy threw his arms around him and held him in a bear hug. There was a loud bang, and they both fell. Flarence looked at the hole that had been torn in his leg just below the knee. Roy had a similar wound. He looked toward the bed and saw a wisp of smoke rising from the barrel of the shotgun. "You're hurting more than you're helping," shouted Flarence as he deconstructed the legs of the bed so the mattress fell on top of Gil.

Flarence rolled away to give his leg time to heal. As he did, the metal shards burst from Roy's chest and flew to the mattress. Gil wailed as the bullets passed through it, but there was no way to know how injured he was. The bullets returned to Roy's chest as Flarence stood up. He prepared to attack again but was caught off guard when the Stakehail Colt was torn from his hand. Mohinaux entered the room and caught the gun, as well as the icicle that had been stuck in the wall. He met Roy in a flying tackle, wrapping one arm around his chest and driving the icicle into his stomach with the other. As they hit the ground, Mohinaux deconstructed the floor, and they fell to the first floor. Flarence deconstructed the floor below his feet, and when he landed, he saw Mohinaux driving the icicle deep into Roy's stomach. Roy pushed him off, and the two rolled away from each other. Mohinaux released the cylinder and tilted the gun up, catching three icicles as they fell out. Fluid flowed from the wound he had just inflicted.

Flarence realized Mohinaux was focused on the icicle buried deep in Roy's body, increasing its temperature until it melted. Roy squirmed, uncomfortable with the liquid sloshing inside him. Then Mohinaux lunged and drove another icicle into Roy's chest, which he also melted at once. Roy was stumbling around the house like a drunk. He tripped and fell forward. Mohinaux leaped onto his back and drove another icicle into him, aiming for his liver. Roy flopped down and grabbed a table to hold himself on his knees as Mohinaux hopped off his back.

"You're strong and fast, but Enchanted blood cells are still blood cells, and they react the same way as everyone else's," said Mohinaux as he struck Roy in the throat with the last icicle, melting it as it punctured his skin. Roy thrashed weakly for a moment and then collapsed.

The sounds of fighting continued in the distance, but Flarence couldn't turn away until he could confirm that Roy was once again dead. As he searched for something sharp to decapitate him with, the Old Ticker entered the room.

Flarence ran at him. The Old Ticker fired a heat spell. It hurt but Flarence still had enough momentum to hit the Old Ticker in the jaw with the Wrist Cannon. Both of them fell as Soleil entered, his pants stained with thick ooze.

"What did you do to her?" Soleil bellowed.

"Darren, help," shouted the Old Ticker as he scampered across the floor to avoid the dart Soleil threw at him.

In a moment, Darren was also in the room. As he assessed the scene, Claire came up from behind and drove her elbow into his spine. The Old Ticker holstered his gun and crawled to Roy. He grabbed an ankle with one hand and reached out to Darren with the other. "Get us out of here!"

Darren lunged at the Old Ticker, and their hands met. The three of them vanished. Flarence, Claire, Mohinaux, and Soleil stood still with their guard up, all of them expecting Darren to reappear. But as time passed and he didn't, they relaxed. Flarence noticed a dark spot on Claire's scarf. "Are you all right?"

She lowered her scarf to reveal a cut lip and a bruise on her chin. "A little banged up, but I'll be fine."

"Amanda's dead," said Soleil. Flarence and Claire turned to him as he gestured to his pants. "The Old Ticker turned her into . . . this. It's like he performed a deconstruction spell on her body. Her skin, bones, organs—everything just turned to mush. It was almost instantaneous. One moment she was screaming and the next she was a puddle."

Neither Flarence nor Claire knew what to say. In the living room, Emma was sobbing over Stewart's body while Tymbir had a hand on her shoulder. Gil had a shirt wrapped around his arm where the bullets had struck him.

"I'm sorry, Emma," said Soleil. "Tonight was a failure in every way."

"Not entirely," said Flarence. "Dad found Inspector R.E.D.'s weakness. He stabbed him with my icicles and then melted them."

"I should have thought of it sooner," said Mohinaux. "You can't expose blood cells to pure water. They soak it up like tiny sponges and swell until they burst. I figured if Inspector R.E.D. got his power from Darren's Enchanted blood, then destroying that blood would take away his powers."

"So it's over," said Gil.

"I wish we could say that," said Soleil, "but when Darren fled, he took Inspector R.E.D.'s body with him."

Gil moved a dry part of the shirt over his wound. "Who's Darren? And what does it matter? You said Roy was down and out."

"Coming back is kind of his thing," said Flarence.

—6—

DARREN

Darren was upset about not being able to kill Tymbir but was hopeful he had found a valuable ally. While he had no confidence that one freak had a chance of overcoming three Genies and Razor Punk, he had been impressed by what the stranger could do.

"One of the men in the barn was the one who took my gun," said Dr. Wicker. "I'm going to need your help getting it back."

"We can worry about that later," said Darren. "Right now, we have other work to do. I brought this guy to life before and I'll probably be able to do it again." Darren walked to a shelf that was charred and barely staying upright.

"This is the place I burned," said Dr. Wicker.

"I figured we'd be alone here," said Darren. "I just hope you didn't destroy everything." He kicked debris out of the way and unearthed a syringe. It was covered in dust, and the needle was slightly bent, but the plunger still worked.

Dr. Wicker and Darren sat across from each other with Roy between them. Darren rolled up his sleeve and worked the lace off his right shoe, then looped it around his arm, grabbed one end in his teeth, and pulled it into a tight knot with his other hand. He tapped his arm and waited for the vein to be easier to see. "I was trying to make the corpse look like me," he explained before Dr. Wicker asked what he was doing, "but I was overzealous and figured I should give him some fresh blood—my blood—to make it appear more realistic. The blood brought him back to life and turned him into, well, whatever he is now."

"How much do you think he needs?" asked Dr. Wicker.

"How should I know? I don't have this down to a science. I revived him by accident last time, and I didn't keep track of how long it took or how much blood I used."

"Well, whatever you're doing, make it quick. If we hurry back to the barn, we can recover my gun and you can kill that Tymbir guy you're always talking about."

"We're not going anywhere until you tell me what you're doing. I was fine on my own, but if you insist on being involved, I deserve to know how you got roped into all this. When you burned this place down, you killed everyone inside, including Mike, Danny, Juan, and Josh. You even tried to kill me."

"I guess I do owe you an explanation." Dr. Wicker winced as the needle punctured Darren's skin.

"Don't tell me you can't stand the sight of blood," said Darren as he placed the tip against the dead man's neck.

"Blood is fine. I just don't like needles."

Darren took his time penetrating the corpse's skin, and depressed the plunger slowly. "Get on with your story or you'll be here all day watching this. I'm guessing Soleil called you the Old Ticker because you have a clock on your mask. What's the deal with that?"

"It's actually a graphic of a particle accelerator, with the lines pointing to the positions of two particles on a collision course. The resemblance to a clock approaching midnight is a reference to the Doomsday Clock. Nuclear behavior is a part of my research."

Darren shook his head. "I didn't exactly pay attention in school. Maybe I would have if I ever showed up."

Dr. Wicker brushed his hands over the symbols on his shirt. "Then I guess you don't know anything about Quantum Field Theory either."

Darren shook his head as he drove the needle into his skin again, forcing it as far as it would go.

"All right, well, do you know about atoms?"

"Sure," said Darren. He tried to recall one of the times he'd been in Tyrell's room while he was doing his homework. "Protons, right?"

"That's an outrageously oversimplified description. Are you aware protons are composed of smaller"—he paused and drummed his fingers on the floor—"things?"

"No, I'm not, but those 'smaller things' better be important because if you don't get to the point soon, some of your blood's going in this guy too."

"The smaller things are called elementary particles, which are very important, and so are other things called bosons. It's what these symbols represent. If I know my history, most of the puzzle has been put together, but this piece is still missing." He pointed to the χ symbol on his chest.

"Of course, X," said Darren. "The letter that makes everything sound cool."

"It's not an X. It's the Greek symbol, Chi. The Chi boson won't be known for some time. They're evasive because they have a remarkable transitional ability. Essentially, this one field is in a constant state of flux, continuously merging with the others."

"Again, I dropped out of high school," Darren interrupted.

"Right, sorry." Dr. Wicker scratched his head. "The important thing is that generating Chi bosons and controlling their path of interaction results in the ability to manipulate forces. Machines will eventually be designed which can use Chi bosons to produce gravitons and make objects heavier or lighter." He ran his hand over his mask, stroking it like a beard. "They can also be weaponized. Those small things I mentioned that are inside protons are called gluons and quarks. Chi control can be used to influence them and alter an atom's stability, making them fissile. That means pretty much anything could be used to develop nuclear bombs. This discovery pushed the Doomsday Clock very close to midnight, where it remained for years."

Most of the information was still beyond Darren's understanding, but he perked up at the word "bomb." "If you can make nukes, then why're you walking around with those puny guns?"

"Most of the machines controlling Chi activity were huge. I focused on making the technology smaller. My goal was to produce a portable Chi controller."

The body between them twitched, and Darren scooted away from it. The last time the body regained consciousness, it had freaked out. Then again, the corpse had been fighting Flarence at the time. Darren couldn't blame the guy for panicking after pulling three icicles out of his head. For the moment, the body just rotated a shoulder and then went still again.

Darren sat near the corpse but Dr. Wicker paced about the room as he spoke. "I developed a schematic for such a device but had some trouble getting funding to make it a reality. There were plenty of debates about the use of weaponized Chi tech, so most universities and laboratories were too afraid of public backlash to fund research on the subject. There were a few places out of the public eye, though. I was contacted by a representative of the army named General Broadsord who knew about my idea, and after talking to some people, he got me onto a military base. I thought I'd be working with a large team, but instead, I found myself with only one partner named Eleanor Trikeye."

He paused and absent-mindedly caressed his gun as he stared at the wall. "Ellie was a brilliant scientist, and it didn't take long for us to become friends. Successfully developing a portable weapon didn't happen immediately, but we had some success. Our first useful invention was called the De-bond Cannon, which altered intermolecular forces and broke chemical bonds. Anything in their line of fire was instantly turned to dust. Ellie was very insistent that our inventions be kept on American bases to only be used for defense and never brought into a battlefield. We were both naive enough to believe her request had been taken to heart, but the De-bond Cannons actually had been sent into battle and used to obliterate buildings."

"How could you not have known your inventions were being used as weapons of mass destruction?"

Dr. Wicker gave Darren a condescending look, as if he thought the answer should be obvious. "We were in an arms race. Advancements in Chi tech established America as a global superpower, and the military took no chances of our research being leaked. Ellie and

I lived in a heavily guarded bunker, and Broadsord kept a close eye on us. Our bedrooms and bathroom were in that bunker. Meals were brought to us. When we began building a machine, we made a list of what we needed, and the parts were delivered piece by piece. We weren't allowed to contact anyone without the appropriate security clearance, which was particularly hard on Ellie who was married and had two children. She tried to send messages to her husband but was caught and disciplined every time."

Dr. Wicker sighed and rubbed his forehead. "It turned out she didn't need to contact them. They found a way to her. Unfortunately, they did it in the worst way possible. Ellie's son became a journalist and produced a documentary which captured the De-bond Cannons in action. Don't ask me for details on that war. I wasn't told then and I don't care now. However, I eventually got around to seeing the film. It was brutal. The tanks were meant to destroy vehicles, but a lot of people were caught in the line of fire and were liquefied, just like that girl on the farm."

"You liquefied a girl while we were on that farm?" said Darren. "That's messed up."

Dr. Wicker chuckled. "A moment ago, you were looking down on me for getting squeamish around needles, and now you don't want me talking about deconstructing a person you didn't even know."

Darren broadened his shoulders and stabbed himself with the syringe. "We're all uncomfortable with something." Dr. Wicker cringed as Darren stabbed himself harder and faster. "I can keep this up all day, Wicker. Rapid healing is one my powers."

"All right, all right! I won't bring it up again, just knock it off." Darren lowered the syringe, and the holes in his chest closed. The corpse between them stirred again and emitted a faint grunt but didn't fully wake up, and Darren motioned for Dr. Wicker to continue.

"Anyway, the documentary Ellie's son made went global. Many people were outraged, and the use of Chi tech was widely considered a war crime. Eventually, all the weapons Ellie and I made were dismantled, and the bunker was abandoned. But Ellie didn't fare too well afterward. Her husband, her son, me—we all tried to comfort her, but the documentary hit her pretty hard. One day she snapped. Her husband found her with a shotgun resting against what remained of her blown-off head."

Before he could stop himself, Darren scoffed, and Dr. Wicker looked at him quizzically. "Sorry," said Darren, "I just hate hearing about people taking the easy way out."

"You're right to apologize, because it wasn't the easy way out. As far as I'm concerned, Ellie's death was not suicide; she was crucified. For years after the documentary, we were both constantly ridiculed on talk shows and news programs. We were treated as terrorists, and on more than one occasion, both Ellie and I were attacked by angry activists. Exposure to all that torment drove her to believe the hype. She was convinced that she was responsible for the deaths of hundreds, and was unable to forgive herself."

"Clearly you forgave yourself." Darren nodded at the revolver. "You even kept going."

Dr. Wicker paced faster and waved his arms as he spoke. "I never forgave myself for anything because I have nothing to feel sorry for. The weapons I created were used in war, but foreign militias were not the enemy. The true enemies were ignorance and fear of the unknown. The soldiers had no idea how the weapons worked or what they were capable of. They just fired because they were told to.

"The protesters and newscasters did what they called 'research.' They looked up information on the internet and then spoke as if they were professionals. They knew nothing of my work, Ellie's work, or the work of any other great mind that came before us. My employment didn't end because my actions were evil. It ended because in the future, the world is full of frightened, melodramatic morons. Everyone got caught up with the death and destruction, but nobody ever considered what our weapons meant for the future of physics. It took years for me to find my way back to a position where I could continue my studies."

"Really? If it was that bad, I'm amazed you were able to find your way back at all."

"I found a job at a university," said Dr. Wicker with a groan. "None of the students were particularly brilliant and seemed to be more interested in hearing my side of the story regarding weaponized Chi tech than actually learning." He chuckled and shook his head. "They didn't want to learn and so I didn't teach them. I made up ridiculous stories about life in the bunker and did a half-assed job grading their assignments. The teaching was mostly to keep up appearances anyway.

"Being a close friend of Ellie resulted in me being a close friend of her family, particularly the journalist son. The boy was just as pathetic as all the others who hopped on the bandwagon and protested Chi tech, but he had worth. While conducting research for his documentary, he discovered things about Broadsord, things he didn't include in the film, things I could use as leverage. I blackmailed Broadsord and forced him to allow me access to a research facility that was not quite as advanced as the bunker but still impressive. It was there that I perfected the revolvers I carry today."

"It doesn't sound like you should be calling anyone else a moron," said Darren. "Your research was halted because it was used to make weapons. Why would you want to keep it up?"

"You're just like them," said Dr. Wicker. "You're focusing on the destruction which is preventing you from seeing the bigger picture. The key word here is not death but control." He removed the gun from its holster. "This handheld device can generate electricity, regulate temperature, and break down solid objects. Regardless of public opinion, I could not turn my back on this project, especially when there was still so much more to discover. I was working in the lab late one night and I had an Earth-shattering idea. If my hypothesis was correct, it would be the crowning point of my career, and possibly the greatest discovery of my generation. You've seen what my guns are capable of, but under just the right conditions and utilization of a much larger machine, Chi control can lead to an even more astounding power."

"Let me guess," said Darren. "It can mess with time."

"Exactly!" shouted Dr. Wicker. "I had a lot of fun dropping that bombshell on Broadsord, as well as the rest of the world. Before I used the time machine, I tested my gun. I went after some of the most outspoken protesters of Chi tech and made them realize just how little they understood about my devices."

"I'm guessing that means you killed them," said Darren.

"Well, I needed an attention-grabber," said Dr. Wicker. "Nothing grabs public attention like a good crime spree. I didn't just murder the people who were instrumental in blocking my research. I schooled them in what my weapons could do, and then I escaped to the twenty-first century."

"But it wasn't your last crime. You still haven't explained how your list fits into all this."

The corpse writhed on the floor like a child awakened by an alarm clock. "That's a story for another time," said Dr. Wicker as he stopped pacing.

Darren moved closer to the body and leaned over it. "Do you know who you are?"

The corpse, more collected than the last time he was revived, rose to his feet. He looked around the room, examined his hands and clothes. He saw the nametag on his lab coat. "Inspector R.E.D." He spoke slowly and softly. "I'm . . . I'm . . . ."

Darren finished for him. "You're back from the dead."

SOLEIL

"I know you're trying to help and I appreciate it, but if you tell me to take a deep breath one more time, I'm going to rip your tongue out." Soleil moved the air to create a gentle breeze while Emma sat across from him in his bedroom, surrounded by his house plants. They were both cross-legged, and Soleil was trying to walk her through breathing exercises.

"Emma, please try to work with me. I brought you here to help you cope with the stress of what happened at the barn. I put a lot of work into making this room feel tranquil. The plants are a reminder that in spite of the recent deaths, life is constantly thriving all around us. Now once again, take a deep breath in."

Emma screamed and stood up. "I don't want to take deep breaths and think about plants right now. I want a bottle of whiskey."

"I'm not going to give you alcohol when you're pregnant."

"I don't want to drink it. I want to set it on fire. You want to help me cope with stress? Watching something burn will help take my mind off things, and don't tell me that's messed up. My husband was killed by a zombie, who your father killed with an ice gun, and you walked off a lawnmower blade through the heart. I'm the normal one here."

"Inspector R.E.D. isn't a zombie; he's an Enchanted corpse," Soleil called out as Emma stormed down the stairs. He decided to give her time to decompress but ran after her when he heard a commotion in the dining area. He found her throwing chairs against the wall and overturning tables. "What are you doing?" he shouted over the noise. He tried to hold her still but she struggled out of his grasp and continued her assault on the furniture. "Emma, you need to meet me halfway here. Breathing exercises and meditation isn't your thing. I get that, but I can't let you wreck my house."

"Can't you just work your magic and put the furniture back together?"

"That's not the point. Just calm down for a second and tell me what you want to do."

Emma threw a salt shaker across the room. "Fine, I want to keep smashing things. I want to hit people. I want to burn down this house. I want to . . . ." She put a hand to her head and started to stumble. Soleil caught her and eased her into an unbroken chair.

"Just sit tight for a minute. I'll get you some water." He started to walk away but Emma caught his wrist.

"I want to visit Gil."

"All right, give me a minute to find him. You just sit there and try to relax, and don't forget to take . . ."

"Don't you dare say deep breaths."

Soleil slumped in a chair to perform an astral projection. He found Gil in his house throwing clothes into a suitcase on the bed. Next to the suitcase was the shotgun he had used when Roy attacked him. "If you want to talk to him, we'd better move fast," said Soleil as he sat up. "It looks like he's getting ready for a long vacation.

Gil was too preoccupied with trying to close the bulging suitcase to hear them arrive. "Dad is supposed to be watching you," said Soleil. Gil went for the gun and Soleil deconstructed it.

Gil fell to his knees and sifted his hands through what remained of the gun. "Give it back. He's coming for me. I need to protect myself. I need to get away from here."

"Relax, Gil," said Soleil. "Nobody's going to hurt you."

"Speak for yourself," said Emma as she stepped toward Gil and kicked him in the face. As he rubbed his jaw, she jumped on top of him, grabbed his hair, and pounded his head on the floor.

Mohinaux came in. "I heard the ruckus. What's going on?"

"It looks like Gil was planning to leave," said Soleil.

"I'm aware," said Mohinaux. "I agree that he should get away for a while. It's not safe for him here.

Emma rolled off Gil. "Is this about Stewart?" he asked as Mohinaux helped him up. "Look, I'm sorry he died, but we need to get out of here. We need to get as far away from this city as possible."

"You're not going anywhere," said Emma. She picked up his suitcase and hurled it toward a window, but Soleil summoned the suitcase back to the mattress before it could crash through the glass.

"Emma," said Soleil, "I know you've been through a lot, and I want to help you, but again, I'm not going to let you trash a house."

Gil got to work repacking the suitcase. "Stewart was in more trouble than you know, Emma. Roy had dirt on us, and I'm not just talking about the conditions at the factory. I'm in deep with dangerous people. If anything, you should be glad your husband's problems ended before you discovered the truth."

"What kind of people?" asked Emma. "How dangerous?"

"That's information I'd prefer to take to my grave," said Gil.

"Roy's hell-bent on sending you there as soon as possible," Emma answered. "You might as well clear your conscious before it happens."

"No dice," said Gil. "On the off chance I get away from Roy and pay off my debts, I'd prefer it if as few people knew about my private life as possible. Besides, knowing the truth would tarnish your memory of Stewart."

"Fine, whatever." Emma sat on the bed. "I never took Stewart for a saint. I know everyone has secrets, but he deserved better than that."

"Then I guess he got less than he deserved," said Gil. "Sucked to be him. Now if you don't mind, I need to get out of this city before the freaks come back."

"Don't call them freaks," said Soleil. "One of them is a Genie, just like me. And you're not going anywhere. Like I said, nobody's going to hurt you."

"Inspector R.E.D. was able to kill Stewart even when we were all working together to protect him," said Mohinaux. "If he's teamed up with Darren and the Old Ticker, we can't guarantee Gil's safety. They could come crashing through these walls at any minute just like when Emma was attacked."

"Roy didn't attack me," said Emma. "Flarence and Stu are about the same size, and they both wear suits. It was a case of mistaken identity."

"That's right," said Soleil. "He didn't kill you in your house. He didn't lay a finger on you in the barn, either. In fact, he hesitated before killing Stewart in front of you. He still cares about you. Working together may be their vulnerability rather than their strength. Dad, meet me at Flarence's cafe, and bring Gil with you."

"I'm not letting you do that weird mental travel thing to me again," said Emma with her arms across her chest, "and I'm definitely not going anywhere with Gil."

She tried to walk out of the room but Soleil grabbed her. "Sorry, Emma, but we still need you a little longer."

FLARENCE

Claire stood in front of a table with different objects on it. Flarence had deconstructed some leather belts and reformed them into a holster for the Old Ticker's gun. "Light the bulb," he said. Claire whipped the gun out of the holster, clicked the thumb switch twice, and fired an electrocution spell at the bulb on the table to light it up. "Melt the ice," said Flarence. She selected another chamber and fired a heat spell at the cube. "Summon the penny," said Flarence. Claire accidentally selected the invisibility spell, and the penny vanished.

"Damn it," she said as she shoved the gun back in the holster. "All the chambers look the same. It would help if we put some labels on them."

"If you're in a fight, you can't be checking your selection before you shoot," said Flarence. "The Old Ticker has all the chambers' abilities memorized. If you take him on, you need to be just as fast as him with your spell selection." He reformed and refroze the ice cube. "Try again."

"I thought you were more into razor blades anyway," said Tymbir.

"Until recently, Flarence and I spent most of our time tracking down runaways and common criminals," said Claire. "We have a whole new level of enemies now, and I'd like to be able to attack from a distance."

"All right," said Flarence, "once again, try to summon the penny to the fridge."

Claire aimed the gun and selected another chamber. When she fired, the penny didn't melt or become encased in ice. She grinned and swept the gun across the room. A moment after she squeezed the trigger, Soleil appeared in front of the refrigerator. The penny rose from the table and cut his ear as it flew past his head. "Sorry," said Claire.

"The gun is loaded with six spells," said Flarence, counting them off on his fingers. "There's heating, freezing, electrocution, deconstruction, summoning, and invisibility."

Claire selected a different chamber and fired at a wall. A small ring became transparent, allowing a peek into Flarence's bedroom. "The invisibility spell only applies to the diameter of the beam, though. It can't make a whole person invisible, but I'm thinking it could be useful to find someone if they're hiding behind something."

"I'm glad you're getting comfortable with the Old Ticker's weapon," said Soleil, "but we may not have to fight them."

"We each have something they want," said Flarence. "Inspector R.E.D. wants Gil, Darren wants Tymbir, and I'm pretty sure the Old Ticker wants his gun back. They'll come at us with everything they've got."

"I tried to talk Darren out of killing Tymbir before, and I'm going to try again," said Soleil. "I also brought Emma because I think she can talk Inspector R.E.D. out of killing Gil."

"No, you brought me here because you weren't listening," said Emma. "I told you: I'm done with all this."

"But Inspector R.E.D. isn't done," said Soleil. "Darren and I have history, and when he shows up, I can try to get through to him. You can get through to your friend."

"We're way past the point of talking," said Flarence.

"I have to believe Darren isn't beyond redemption," said Soleil, "and the same goes for Inspector R.E.D."

"We were all on the farm together last night," said Gil. "You saw that freak shred my brother's heart and try to do the same to me."

"Stop calling people like us freaks," said Soleil. "And Claire, back me up on this. You don't want to kill anybody, do you?"

"You know I don't," said Claire, "and I want to believe that we can get through to Darren for Tyrell's sake, but we're dealing with very dangerous people right now, and I can't afford to let my guard down. I won't take the first shot, but if it looks like there's going to be trouble, I won't hesitate to use this gun."

"And trust me" said Tymbir, "Razor Punk will have to use that gun. You and Emma might be able to talk to Darren and Inspector R.E.D., but the Old Ticker is unaccounted for. If things don't go his way, there's going to be another brawl, and even with the Student on your side, you had trouble last night."

"Okay, someone really needs to give me a nickname," said Flarence.

Soleil shot him an annoyed look.

"What?" said Flarence. "Claire is Razor Punk, Dad is the Student, Roy is Inspector R.E.D., and, well, what's-his-name is the Old Ticker. From now on, you can call me . . . um, give me a minute."

"We'll talk about that back at my cafe," said Soleil.

"We can't go back to your cafe," said Claire. "It's quiet but there could be a chain reaction. A deconstructed wall followed by a mis-fired heat spell and the forest is up in flames. If we stay here, a deconstruction spell could take a few floors of this building down."

"No matter what, there's going to be a risk of collateral damage," said Tymbir. "Where are we supposed to go, a cave?"

"That's fine by me," said Mohinaux.

—7—

DARREN

"And now Gil Saucen is the only one left," said Roy. The three men were sitting on the floor, explaining what had brought them together. Dr. Wicker recounted his life's events but only as far as he'd gone with Darren, and no explanation of his list. Since the doctor was concealing information, Darren did not feel guilty doing the same. He explained how he'd brought Roy back to life but not how he had gotten his powers, fearing that Dr. Wicker would demand to be Enchanted if he knew how easy it was for magical abilities to be shared. Even if Dr. Wicker was on their side, he still seemed shady, and Darren did not trust him enough to give him powers.

"Speed is important for all of us," said Dr. Wicker. "The Genie family could be watching us right now with astral projections."

"You should be safe," explained Darren. "They can only spy on you if they have something specific to focus on, and they don't know much about you. I'm safe because I'm a Genie as well, and having abilities offers a natural protection from magical attacks. Roy, you're kind of a wild card. I don't know exactly how things work for you, but you're packed full of Enchanted blood, which might shield you from magic."

"I'm not safe from them entirely," said Roy. "The Student found a way to kill me."

"Working together will improve our chances," said Darren, "but we're still outnumbered. Tymbir is just a human, but he's an ex-cop and he's a fighter. Razor Punk doesn't have powers either, but I've seen her take on a Genie before, and believe me when I say she's very good at it. We're going to need to separate our targets from their bodyguards."

"If we give you an opening to get your hands on Gil or Tymbir, could you summon him back to this apartment?" asked Dr. Wicker.

"Easily," said Darren, "but Soleil and Flarence can track them with their astral projections. Once we isolate one of them, we won't be able to hide for very long.

"We need to find a place where the Genies can't use their summoning spell," said Roy.

"There's always something to summon to," said Darren. "Even if we go to a large, empty room, they could just summon their bodies to a wall."

"I doubt that when Flarence uses his revolver, he's spontaneously creating icicles," said Dr. Wicker. "Instead, he must be drawing in humidity from the air and instantly freezing it. Darren, am I right in assuming you can do the same thing?"

"Sure, I can freeze water. I can freeze and boil anything on demand."

"Then it's a good thing we're in Chicago," said Dr. Wicker. "You create a sheet of ice in Lake Michigan large enough to summon to."

"But if Darren can summon us to the ice raft, then the other Genies would be able to do the same thing," said Roy. "It wouldn't offer any protection."

"We may be able to stand on the water even if it isn't frozen," said Dr. Wicker. "Darren, if you can control the temperature of a liquid, can you also control its surface tension? If you can, then once we get to the lake you can melt the ice so Soleil and Flarence can't follow us, and replace it with a giant water bead firm enough for us to stand on."

"I like the idea," said Darren. "The problem is my powers require focus. If I can successfully make the water bead, I'll be too engaged on maintaining it to concentrate on anything else. What's to stop one of them from refreezing the water once we melt our ice sheet?"

"Me," said Dr. Wicker. "I can set my gun to heat. It will allow me to keep the water melted while Inspector R.E.D. finishes the job."

"Do you really think that gun will overrule their magic?" asked Roy.

"I'll admit it's a bit of a gamble," said Dr. Wicker. "If it doesn't, then Darren can summon us back to this apartment. I think it's our best shot, though."

SOLEIL

The dank, earthy smell of the cave and the dull glow of the fluorescent orbs made Emma keel over and vomit moments after the group arrived. Soleil held her hair back as she heaved and swore.

"You know, Soleil, if you had killed Darren when I told you to, there wouldn't have been anyone around to revive Inspector R.E.D., and things would be a little easier now," said Mohinaux.

"Don't put all the blame on him," said Flarence. "I had a chance to kill Darren before and failed. I won't make that mistake again. By the way, what do you think of calling me the Flare?"

Soleil helped Emma back to her feet. "I'm not sorry for trying to reason with Darren," he said, "and nobody's going to start calling you the Flare."

"Give it some time," said Flarence. "It might grow on you."

Emma spat on the floor. "It's the dumbest thing I've ever heard."

"Come on, it goes with my name: Flarence, the Flare."

"But you don't even use fire," said Claire. "In fact, your gun shoots ice. It's the opposite of a flare gun."

"Then I'll make some kind of enhanced flare gun," said Flarence. "It shouldn't be too hard."

"It wouldn't make sense to base your nickname off of just one weapon when you have two other completely different ones," said Claire. "Instead of making something new, try to combine what you already have."

"All right. I use electricity and ice. I've got it: I'm Glacial Lightning!"

"No, you're not," said Tymbir, who had gone to Emma's side. She was still heaving lightly. "Are you all right?"

"I'll be fine," said Emma. "We're hopefully just going to talk, right? As long as it's just talking, I'll be fine."

"I'm telling you that's not how this is going to go down," said Tymbir. "Darren's been out for blood since the day we met, and he has no reason to suddenly become diplomatic. I'm all for luring them into a small space away from the public, but Emma, Gil, and I can't stay here when things get violent."

"I'll give you an area of refuge," said Mohinaux. A section of a wall collapsed, providing entry to a tunnel. Along the tunnel walls, more orbs began to glow. "Back when creating and killing monsters was my hobby, I kept the carcasses, preserved them, and stored them in this cave. I suppose you could say they're my trophies. You three can stand by this tunnel, and the second you feel you're in danger, I want you to run down it and find a place to hide."

Soleil went to the mouth of the tunnel. "Why didn't you tell me you kept the bodies? I mean, I've enjoyed going through your journal, but it'd be nice to compare the real things to your sketches."

"It isn't something I like showing off," said Mohinaux. "I'm not proud of keeping it around, but I can't bring myself to get rid of them either."

Emma wiped her chin with her sleeve. "Focus, please."

"I'm sorry," said Soleil, "and I know it isn't an ideal situation."

"No, it isn't," said Emma. "You drag me and my dead fiance's douchebag brother into a cave as bait for a zombie attack and my area of refuge is a crypt for monsters. This stopped being an ideal situation a long time ago."

"Inspector R.E.D. isn't a zombie," said Flarence. "He's an Enchanted corpse."

Emma stepped toward Flarence and looked as if she was about to hit him, but she slipped on her vomit. For a moment, it looked like she was going to burst into tears. Tymbir helped her and walked her toward the tunnel.

"What if you all die down here while we're hiding," said Emma. "Not that I'll feel particularly bad if you all die horribly, but then we'll be stuck having to dig ourselves out."

A rustling was audible in the distance, and when Soleil looked down the tunnel, he saw a speck of light at the end. "There," said Mohinaux, "now you can walk out of here instead of digging out."

A sketch from Mohinaux's journal came to Soleil's mind. "Speaking of monsters," he said, "maybe a living one would make the crypt a better shelter." He loosened the earth on the dome's ceiling and sifted through the pile that fell until he found an earthworm and laid it near the path to the crypt. "If there's trouble, I'll create a Hydra. It'll block the tunnel and buy you some time."

"The Hydra was an Enchanted worm?" said Claire. "I figured it would be some kind of snake or lizard."

"That might have been more interesting," said Mohinaux, "but no. When I Enchanted an earthworm, it grew enormous. A strong, dumb soldier trying to kill it couldn't seem to think of anything other than hacking through its body, but the lopped off sections were still alive and quickly grew to their original size. As the story was retold, it eventually changed to make it sound like the monster's head was cut off and two took its place."

"So how are we supposed to kill it?" said Gil.

"Crushing it will work," said Mohinaux, "and so will burning it or bleeding it. Basically, do whatever you want other than cutting it into pieces."

"How dangerous is it?" asked Claire.

Mohinaux shrugged. "The worm doesn't grow fangs or claws or anything like that, and it's mostly docile, but it will try to smother attackers if it feels threatened."

"Is it going to know we're on its side?" asked Tymbir.

"No," said Soleil, "so the second you see the worm growing, I want you, Emma, and Gil to run down that tunnel as fast as you can."

There was a rustling overhead. Soleil took two vials from his poncho. The others drew their weapons as well. Claire held a razor blade in one hand and the spellcasting revolver in the other. She selected a chamber and fired at the opposite wall. A moment later, three holes formed in the roof of the cave and three men arrived in a triangle, Darren in front with Inspector R.E.D. on his left and the Old Ticker on his right, each bathed in a pillar of light. There was another distant rumbling, and the light was blotted out as the entry tunnels caved in. "You're outnumbered, Darren," said Soleil. "Put the saw down. We can still solve this without more people being hurt."

"No we can't," said Darren. "The damage has been done. The rest of Tymbir's gang is already dead. Even if I give up now and let him live, he'll just start from scratch and build a new team to hunt me down. You're not human either, so you better believe they'll do the same to you."

"Tymbir isn't the first to challenge people like us," said Soleil. "You're new to this. There have been other groups, gangs, cults, orders, whatever you want to call them, made up of people who found out about our powers and tried to kill us, but we're still here because we can take anything anyone throws at us, and we outlive them by eons. You don't have to murder Tymbir to get revenge. Just keep your head down and nature will do the job for you."

"Maybe you're all right spending decades living alone in a beat-up old house, but I'm not. My family lived in a slum for years, and I'm sick of it. I'm not just a bum anymore standing on a corner begging strangers to drop pennies. I'm better than that now."

Roy, apparently in no mood to talk, lunged at Gil. Soleil wasn't ready, but Claire's quick trigger finger fired, and Roy was thrown back, his body summoned to the wall of the cave. Before he could get up, Claire fired at another section of the wall, ready to summon him again.

"I'd like that back," said the Old Ticker

"And I'd like to take your other gun away," said Mohinaux.

"It almost sounds like you're afraid of me," said the Old Ticker. "Maybe it's because if people like Tymbir had my gun, they might actually have a chance of rising up against people like you. Let's find out how much damage just one gun can bring." He fired, and the collar of Mohinaux's shirt burst into flames. Claire fired back, and the Old Ticker was thrown into a wall of the cave near Roy, who avoided the collision and ran toward Gil again. Claire chased the Old Ticker as Flarence intercepted Roy, and the two tumbled to the floor. Soleil turned and saw Tymbir, Gil, and Emma running to the crypt of monsters. He felt a rush of wind and noticed too late the saw blade flying past. Before he could react, it hit Gil in the back, just above his hip, knocking him down. Tymbir and Emma helped him up, which slowed them down and made them more vulnerable. Soleil turned to face Darren. Out of the corner of his eye, he saw Mohinaux and Flarence teaming up against Roy but was worried that they wouldn't be able to hold him off, especially if Roy tried to run after Gil at his superior speed.

Soleil levitated the worm which hovered for a moment before its body grew longer and fell to the ground. In the blink of an eye, it went from an inch to nearly a foot long, and kept growing. The tip that Soleil guessed was the worm's head rose as the tail snaked down the tunnel toward Tymbir, Gil, and Emma. In the distance, Soleil heard them scream and hoped they were far enough away not to be crushed by the creature's growing body. He turned away from the worm and faced Darren, who was staring in awe at the monster, as were Roy and the Old Ticker.

Flarence was the first to take advantage of the distraction, and shot Roy in the back with the Stakehail Colt. Not to be fooled again, Roy reached for the icicle and pulled it out before Flarence could melt it. Hearing the shot brought Darren out of his trance in time to see Soleil coming at him. Darren kicked him into the Hydra. Its flesh felt tender but its body was firmer than Soleil had expected. He bounced off the Hydra and fell. Darren advanced on him but stopped in his tracks and dove sideways. Soleil realized the danger that was crushing down on him and rolled to his right as the Hydra fell on the spot he'd been at a moment ago. He backed away from the beast, whose body was now a few feet thick and up to Soleil's chest as it lay flat on the floor. The Hydra became thinner and longer as it moved into the cave. If what Mohinaux said was true, it was going to try to crush every one of them. Soleil just hoped that its body was large enough to keep the tunnel blocked as it did so.

The Hydra couldn't scream, but it squirmed in pain as Darren leaped over its body, saw blade in hand after summoning it from the tunnel. The Hydra, cut by the blade as it flew to Darren, was big but not observant, and, acting purely on instinct, it thrashed in the direction the pain had come from even though Darren was no longer there.

As Darren swung the blade, Soleil pivoted to avoid it and dropped a vial. He stomped on it and backed away as a small twister formed. Dirt, shards of glass, and the contents of the vial swirled around Darren. As he inhaled the powder, his muscles relaxed and his legs shook, threatening to collapse beneath him.

His body was resisting the sedative, and the symptoms probably would not last long. Soleil made a fist but before he was close enough to punch, the Hydra's body fell in front of him, with Darren beneath it. In his sedated state, Darren was powerless as the Hydra rose and fell on top of him again, pummeling, suffocating, and crushing him all at once.

Suddenly Soleil heard a sizzling and saw the Hydra's flesh blacken as either Claire or the Old Ticker hit it with a heat spell. The Hydra moved away from Darren and thrashed in the direction the burning beam had come from. As it moved, it hit Soleil in the face, knocking him on his back. When he sat up, he saw Claire fighting with the Old Ticker while Mohinaux and Flarence were battling Inspector R.E.D., but he didn't see Darren anywhere. The Hydra's body was still blocking the tunnel where Tymbir, Emma, and Gil had run, but there was another hole in the cave wall that hadn't been there earlier. Soleil ran down the new tunnel.

He felt foolish for having thought Darren would stay and fight him. Tymbir was his target. Darren had seen Tymbir run down the tunnel before it was blocked, and was now deconstructing the cave's walls to make a new path that would intercept him. Soleil ran as fast as he could, but there were no lights and he crashed into a wall. Darren must have known Soleil would follow him and purposely filled it with twists and turns. Soleil didn't have a flashlight but he did have a vial of nitrocellulose. He pulled it from his poncho and lit it but slowed its reaction time, stabilizing the explosive and turning it into a small torch.

Darren had been thorough in making the tunnel difficult to navigate. Soleil turned left and right so much he felt like he was running through a maze. His makeshift torch was bright enough, but the vial wasn't very big and, though stabilized, wouldn't burn for long. Several turns later, Soleil heard footsteps in the distance. He was getting close. The tunnel joined Tymbir's path. For a moment, he was worried that Mohinaux would be at a disadvantage if he was focused on keeping the orbs lit while in a fight, but then again, he had more control of his powers than Soleil and Flarence combined.

Soleil dropped the vial and stopped focusing on it. The remaining gun cotton flashed and emitted a small puff as it burned up. In the distance, he saw a small ring of light at the end of the tunnel and the outlines of the three people Soleil had tried so hard to protect, along with the image of Darren running toward them. Gil was limping, and Emma was hopping on one leg with her arm around Tymbir's shoulder. Soleil guessed she had not gotten away from the Hydra fast enough and been hurt as it grew.

"I've got you now!" Darren shouted, his booming voice echoing through the tunnel. Tymbir knew he wasn't going to make it out of the cave. He let go of Emma and turned to face his attacker, standing with fists raised and muscles taught, ready to make his last stand.

He didn't get the chance. Supporting Emma down the long tunnel had left him drained and hardly able to put up any sort of fight. Darren didn't slow down and leaped at Tymbir, swinging his saw blade a split second before their bodies collided, sending them both down in a bloody mess.

Soleil stopped running and fell to his knees. Even though he wasn't hurt, the sight left him feeling absolutely defeated. Tymbir's breathing came in short gasps, and even in the dull glow of the lights,

Soleil could see the dark red stain on his chest when Darren rolled off. The blade was also dripping with blood.

"Darren," Soleil whispered, but he couldn't get out any other words. After everything Soleil and his family had done to protect Tymbir, after all the times Soleil had tried to reason with Darren, it was over. Darren had done it. He actually had done it. It was almost too much for Soleil to comprehend.

"I wanted to make him suffer more," said Darren as he got to his feet, "but you made me pretty desperate." He knelt over Tymbir's body and gripped the dying man's shoulders. "That doesn't mean I can't kick him around post-mortem." He summoned his body away from the cave, taking Tymbir with him.

FLARENCE

Mohinaux, not realizing that the Stakehail Colt was out of ammo, had Roy in a headlock and tried to keep him still so Flarence could shoot him. By the time Flarence reloaded, Roy had struggled out of Mohinaux's grip. Things went so much more smoothly, Flarence knew, when Claire had his back and kept track of how many icicles were fired. Now he couldn't see either Claire or the Old Ticker, his view of the other side of the cave blocked by the Hydra. Last he'd seen her, it looked like she was holding her ground. The Old Ticker was more comfortable with his gun, and cycling through the spells kept her at a distance, but Claire's agility and athleticism made up for her lesser familiarity with the weapon. She flipped and darted around to avoid his shots. If she could just get close to the Old Ticker, she could disarm and incapacitate him easily. Flarence hoped she found a way to turn the tide in her favor soon. Even though he had Mohinaux's assistance, Roy was putting up a good fight, and he could really use her help.

Roy was even harder to pin down now that he knew being struck with an icicle meant certain death. He had dodged every shot from

Flarence and increased his strength to break free every time Mohinaux tried to grab him. The Hydra was still blocking the tunnel like it was supposed to, but its body was long enough to be an obstacle for everyone.

Flarence decided he was relying on his gun too much and moved in, hitting Roy in the nose with his Wrist Cannon. He tried to follow with a pistol whip but Roy ducked to avoid it. The Hydra lunged again and sent Flarence and Roy scrambling across the cave floor. But instead of trying to crush them, it drove its head into a wall. Its body became thinner as it expanded, and then thickened as it compressed. The monster had finally had enough and was retreating. It moved fast for a worm and disappeared from the cave quickly. When the last of the Hydra's body receded, Roy ran down the tunnel toward Emma, Gil, and Tymbir. Mohinaux chased after him as Flarence helped Claire.

He became invisible and snuck up behind the Old Ticker, who had his gun set to freeze but missed and created a layer of frost on the cave wall. Flarence landed a solid blow with the Wrist Cannon between the Old Ticker's shoulder blades, bringing him to his knees. Claire ran at her downed opponent, sliding like in a baseball game to kick him in the chest. As he tried to get up, Flarence kicked him unconscious. Claire retrieved the second gun. "I could get used to these," she said.

"If you switch to guns, we can't call you Razor Punk anymore," said Flarence.

"You need to stop obsessing over nicknames," said Claire as she stuck one gun in the holster and the other in her jeans. "I always thought Flarence was a pretty unique name anyway."

Suddenly they heard footsteps and turned to see Mohinaux, Soleil, and Gil enter from the tunnel.

"Emma's gone," said Mohinaux. "Inspector R.E.D. grabbed her and ran off. We'll send projections after her later, find out where he took her."

"I'm guessing he's taking her to a hospital," said Soleil. "It looked like she was hurt. Roy must have taken her and left Gil because helping his friend was more important than revenge."

"What about Darren and Tymbir?" said Flarence.

"They're gone." Soleil cringed as he said it. Mohinaux pulled him close in a one-armed hug and rubbed his back. Soleil's gaze fell on the Old Ticker. "At least something good came out of this. Maybe now we can finally find out what we're dealing with."

"Or you could just kill him," said Gil. "That man is dangerous."

"He can't hurt anyone as long as I have both guns," said Claire, "and the more we find out about him, the better. For all we know, he isn't the only one with spellcasting revolvers."

Soleil grabbed the Old Ticker by the wrists. "Meet me in my room. I know how we can get answers from him."

Soleil disappeared from the cave. Mohinaux held on to Gil and did the same, and Flarence followed with Claire. When they arrived, the Old Ticker was lying on the bed with his shirt and mask off. Soleil separated his bed sheets into strips. He braided them into ropes and used them to bind the Old Ticker's arms and legs. Flarence stepped toward the bed. He had pictured the Old Ticker as being older, but while this man was by no means young, he was in decent shape. His face and chest had some gray hairs, and his belly protruded a little, but generally, it looked like he took care of himself. Flarence stopped assessing the Old Ticker's torso and wondered why he was seeing the torso in the first place. "I understand why you removed his mask, but why did you take his shirt off?"

"I doubt he's going to just spill his guts," said Soleil. "I can get him to talk, but I need his skin exposed. Besides, last time I fought him, I woke up in pain with all my clothes missing."

"Are you planning on exposing his lower half as well?" asked Claire.

"No," said Soleil. "I don't like the guy, but I'm not completely heartless. He can hold on to some dignity, even while we're torturing him."

"Torturing?" said Mohinaux as Soleil carried the Old Ticker out the door.

"Yeah," said Soleil. "Follow me. And on the way out, I'd appreciate it if someone grabbed my broom."

—8—

DARREN

Tymbir stirred and tried to prop himself up on his elbows but slipped. He was cold and shivering, but it was because of the block of ice he was lying on rather than blood loss. He rolled onto his side and slowly found the strength and stability to stand. When he looked around, he could see only the blue sky and the waves spreading out in front of him. Tymbir took in his surroundings, and nearly fell when his eyes met Darren's.

"You're not dead yet," said Darren.

Tymbir looked down at his shirt which was soaked in blood. "You cut me in the cave," he said. He lifted his shirt to look at the wound, but beneath the blood stain, his skin was intact.

"Got you good, didn't I?" said Darren as he raised his arm. A scar was faint and fading quickly, but it was still visible along his wrist and forearm. "I didn't cut you when we were in the cave. I cut myself. I had to cut hard and deep to get the effects I wanted. Lucky for me, the cave wasn't lit very well. When I collided with you, I missed with the saw blade but smeared my blood all over your shirt and whacked you hard in the gut. By the time I rolled off you, my arm was mostly healed, you were gasping for breath, and the stain on your shirt made it look like you were hit. Soleil thinks you're dead. It's just you and me out here."

"Where is here?" asked Tymbir.

"We're on Lake Michigan, far enough offshore to not be seen. Hopefully, there won't be any boats coming by. I've never been deep water fishing, but Atalissa talked a lot about how she loved the smell of fresh-cooked salmon and always wanted to take Tyrell out on the lake someday. Thanks to you, she'll never get the chance." Darren threw the saw blade, purposely missing but scaring Tymbir enough to make him lose his balance. As Darren summoned the blade back to his body, Tymbir struggled to stand up.

"Soleil wouldn't fall for a trick that simple," said Tymbir. "You should have killed me when you had the chance. They'll come for me."

"Maybe Flarence and the Student wouldn't fall for a trick that simple, but Soleil has led a quiet life too long and hasn't seen nearly as much violence as the other Genies. That's made him gullible. In the heat of the battle, he wasn't able to tell the difference between a dead man and an injured one. If you need further assurance, consider that Soleil could summon his body to this ice sheet in seconds if he wanted to. If he knew you were alive, he would've come already."

"Or maybe he does know I'm alive but has other things to worry about," said Tymbir. "Soleil would never abandon his family and friends, leaving them behind in a cave to fight Inspector R.E.D. along with the Old Ticker and the giant worm monster. Abandoning loved ones is your move, not his."

Darren knew he shouldn't let Tymbir get to him, but the comment struck a nerve. "I spent most of my life in a dump that I could barely think of as a home. My loved ones were all I had. Everything I've ever done was to protect the people I cared about."

"But that was a pretty small circle," said Tymbir, gaining confidence now that he saw he was getting to Darren. "That's your problem, Darren. You might have been a good person once, but the only people you cared about were your wife, your son, and a handful of friends. They're all gone now. Once you ran out of people to protect, you focused on finding people to hurt."

Darren refused to lose his temper. He wanted to enjoy Tymbir's last moments. He tossed the saw blade which bounced on the ice and came to a rest near Tymbir's feet. "Do you want me to pick that up?"

"I want you to think about it," said Darren smugly. "I want to know what kind of man you are." His legs spread wide for balance, Tymbir slowly bent over to retrieve the saw blade. Darren didn't try to stop him. "Even if Soleil knows you're alive, it's still just you and me out here. Everyone either thinks you're dead or they're too busy fighting to come and help you. The only weapon on this island is that saw blade and you've seen how fast I heal. You're going to die out here, and once your heart stops beating, I'm going to throw you underwater, compress your lungs so all the air comes out, and then force them to expand again so you'll be weighted and sink to the bottom of the lake.

"Nothing you can do will change the outcome, but I'm offering you a choice as to how you want to react. Option one is to accept your fate. If you toss the saw blade back to me, I'll kill you as quickly as possible. I can't make it painless, but you won't scream. I'll go straight for the throat. Option two is to fight back. You won't win, and instead of going for the death blow immediately, I'll make it long and painful, but you'll go down swinging. What's the more dignified way to go? Does quietly laying down your arms and accepting you've lost to a superior opponent make you feel proud, or does it make you feel like a wimp? Does fighting for your life even in a situation you know you can't win make you feel like a warrior, or does it make you feel like an idiot?"

For a moment it looked like Tymbir's face softened. Was it a moment of weakness? Was it a look of acceptance? Darren wanted a fight but would keep his word if Tymbir tossed the blade back to him. He didn't toss it back, though. He lifted it to his own neck. "If I'm going to die, I'll take my own way out."

Darren didn't imagine Tymbir would resort to suicide but knew it was possible, and was prepared for it. He summoned the blade back to his body, and it flew out of Tymbir's hand before he cut his neck too deep. One of the teeth nicked the skin, and a narrow stream of blood flowed down to his collar, but it was nothing life-threatening. "That's not an option," said Darren. Tymbir tried to throw himself into the lake, but Darren froze the water around the island, expanding it so Tymbir only landed on more ice.

"Not. An. Option," Darren repeated, but Tymbir wasn't giving up. He scrambled to the edge of the ice on his hands and knees to try to throw himself underwater again. Darren melted a section of the ice under Tymbir's hand, causing his right arm to fall through. He took his hand from the hole and plunged his head down in its place, blowing the air from his lungs as fast as he could. Darren focused on the water under the island and caused it to rise, creating a jet stream that pushed out Tymbir's head. "You're just making this fun for me," said Darren as Tymbir lay still, coughing while water droplets fell onto and around him.

Tymbir rose to his feet. He didn't try to throw himself off the edge again. He looked Darren in the eye. "Toss the blade back to me."

Darren did as he was asked. "So you're choosing to fight."

Tymbir picked up the blade. "Till the bitter end." He advanced slowly, knowing he couldn't keep his balance on the ice if he ran. He inched close to Darren and circled him with his fists raised. Darren liquefied the ice below Tymbir's left foot, and his leg plunged into the water. He struggled out of the hole, and when he got back on his feet, Darren delivered a punch that sent him sprawling again. He summoned the saw blade to his body and threw it at Tymbir's hand, severing his thumb. Tymbir screamed and held his hand while Darren summoned and threw the blade a few more times, deeply cutting both of Tymbir's legs and his shoulder. The pain was enough to make Tymbir sob. "Thanks for choosing to fight," said Darren. "Seeing you in such a pathetic state makes this extra satisfying."

"I'm not pathetic," said Tymbir, although his voice cracked like a scolded child. He cleared his throat and repeated his words in a purposefully low and gruff voice. He tried to stand again, but the cuts in his legs were too deep, and he settled for resting on his knees.

Darren threw the saw again, this time striking Tymbir in the stomach. It was the first lethal blow he delivered. "Take that out yourself or I'll take it out for you," said Darren.

With a yelp, Tymbir removed the saw blade from his body. There was no stopping the tears now. Darren strode toward Tymbir and forced him onto his back. He put a knee on Tymbir's chest, picked up his saw blade with one hand, and with his free hand drove his fingers into the stomach wound. Tymbir screamed and struggled but Darren held him still. He increased his body weight until he felt Tymbir's ribs crack. Then he removed his fingers from Tymbir's wound and grabbed him by the chin, forcing his head forward so they were looking into each other's eyes.

"I had to deal with a lot of pain to get to this point. The pain of losing Atalissa has been with me every day. So has the pain of abandoning my son so I could focus on getting to you. Soleil got in my way and hurt me as I was hunting you down. I just want you to know that seeing you like this, all alone and crying like a baby while you bleed out, has made every second worthwhile." With his knee still planted, Darren raised the saw blade high above his head and with one final swing slashed Tymbir's throat.

The feeling was surreal. He didn't notice the gurgling as Tymbir tried to gulp in air. In that moment, Darren felt completely at peace. Everything that had happened since the first night he met Soleil in jail, both the good and the bad, didn't matter anymore. He was all alone in the world as he sat on the ice raft, staring out at the calm lake and sky while his jeans soaked in the growing puddle of his enemy's blood.

Darren held his position for a long time, and then he disposed of the body as he had said he would. Even though he was sure Tymbir was dead, he snapped his neck for good measure, and then cut through his spinal cord for fun. Realizing that some of the blood on Tymbir's shirt was his own, he took it off. He didn't want some of his Enchanted blood accidentally seeping into one of Tymbir's wounds and reviving him the way it had revived Roy. He made the shirt weightless and then increased its temperature, making it burst into flames while suspended in midair.

As the ashes blew across the lake, he dragged Tymbir to the edge of the island, submerged his head and neck, and magically forced his lungs to compress. As bubbles rose, Darren pictured the air escaping from Tymbir's nose and mouth, as well as the hole in his neck, and the image made him grin. When all the air was out, he threw the body over the edge, and once it was submerged, he forced the lungs to expand. He watched Tymbir sink until his body was out of view, certain that the fish and other marine life were the only ones who would ever find him.

Having nowhere else to go, Darren summoned his body back to the wrecked apartment and sat on the charred couch. Now that it was over, would Soleil understand, or at least accept what had happened? He imagined the two of them talking about how the situation had played out, and pictured it ending a number of different ways ranging from a peaceful conversation to a brutal outburst.

He thought about what Tymbir had said before dying, how Darren had abandoned his friends in the cave. It was possible that the fight was still going on, and just as likely it had already ended with the deaths of Roy and Dr. Wicker. He wasn't sure how to feel about the doctor, but Roy was a different matter entirely. In a way, he felt that the two of them had a lot in common. Neither had asked for their abilities, but supernatural powers had been forced on both of them. The difference was that Roy had someone left to protect. He had told them about a woman named Emma Saucen before they left the apartment, and Darren assumed she was the woman he had seen in the cave. For all he knew, she was still there.

Darren focused on the name Emma Saucen as he formed an astral projection. To his surprise, his projection was drawn to a hospital bed where Emma lay surrounded by doctors. He figured that meant the fight at the cave was over but wondered who had won. His projection floated to the lobby, figuring that if Soleil had brought

Emma there, he would have stuck around, just as he had after Tyrell was injured in the car crash.

He didn't see anyone he recognized in the lobby, so his projection floated around the hospital perimeter. When he still didn't see anyone, he surveyed the parking lot. Nobody recognizable was hiding behind or sitting in any of the cars. He tried focusing on Roy but couldn't get a reading on him. The Enchanted blood must have been enough of a magical deterrent to keep him safe from being tracked through astral projections.

He decided to find Dr. Wicker. He still didn't consider the doctor a friend, but at the very least, thanks were in order for helping to keep everyone distracted while he finished off Tymbir. His astral projection drifted through the city, but rather than make its way back to Mohinaux's cave, it moved to the nature preserve where Soleil's Cafe was located. His projection hovered away from the trails, away from the cafe, and came to rest in a small clearing in the woods. The scene below his projection confirmed what he had feared: Soleil was not merely upset about Tymbir's death; he had completely lost his mind.

SOLEIL

"Where are we and why are we here?" asked Claire.

"This is where I get the materials for my toxins," said Soleil. He dropped the Old Ticker by the trunk of his Enchanted tree. It barely reached Soleil's shoulders, and was far enough from walking paths that it was seldom seen by people strolling through the nature preserve. Even people who did step off the path and pass by were unlikely to notice anything strange since the tree did not look unusual at a distance. The longest branches were covered in pointed, green needles, which made it look like a young pine. Hidden beneath the needles, closer to the trunk, were berries and flowers of different colors and shapes. Scattered around the tree were piles of dead bugs, as well as small birds and rodents that had tried eating some of the berries, leaves, or bark. Soleil usually cleaned up the dead wildlife around the tree every few days but had been distracted lately and not gotten to it. The Old Ticker groaned and opened his eyes as Soleil moved him close to the tree.

"You're going to answer our questions," said Soleil, "or you're going to get exposed to all my poisons at once."

The only person the Old Ticker could look at directly was Soleil. "Is Gil nearby? Gil, if Inspector R.E.D. hasn't gotten you yet, it's only a matter of time."

"It just so happens that Gil is here, and Inspector R.E.D. isn't going to lay a hand on him. We're keeping him safe," said Soleil.

"Is the girl with my gun also close by?" said the Old Ticker. "I still want that back."

"My name is Razor Punk," said Claire.

"I'll assume the man in the scribbled-on shirt is here somewhere as well," said the Old Ticker.

"Most people call me the Student," said Mohinaux.

"And I'm Glacial Lightning," said Flarence.

"No he's not," said Soleil. He kicked the Old Ticker in the ribs. "From now on, no speaking unless you're spoken to. What's your name?"

The Old Ticker grinned. "You know my name. You're the one who came up with it."

Soleil used the broom handle to shake a branch above the Old Ticker's head. Some of the pine needles fell on his face. "Don't worry about the needles," said Soleil. "They're only dangerous if they puncture your skin." He moved the broom handle deeper. "If you want to get the harder stuff, you have to go to the pollen or the berry juice." As if on cue, a wisp of powder landed just below the Old Ticker's nose. He inhaled some of the pollen and suddenly had difficulty breathing. "I call that the universal allergen," said Soleil. "No matter who breathes that stuff, their airway clamps shut."

"Soleil, we need him alive if we want him to talk," said Flarence.

"He'll live," said Soleil. He held a vial of powder up for everyone to see. "He'd have to inhale this whole thing in order for it to be lethal. The amount he just got will hit him hard but it won't last long." As the Old Ticker struggled to breathe, the skin on his neck and shoulders reddened. "It looks like some of the blue flower pollen got on his skin as well. That stuff will last a while. It triggers pain receptors. Right now, he feels like his neck and shoulders are being burned. As soon as he can take a breath, he'll try to scream."

It wasn't long before the Old Ticker went from being unable to inhale to taking short breaths. He coughed at first but then found the ability to take in a lungful of air and opened his mouth but made no sound. "That won't do you any good," said Soleil. "I'm modifying the sound waves, pushing them to an inaudible frequency. You can scream all you want, but all you'll accomplish is becoming the world's largest dog whistle."

The Old Ticker tried screaming again, but his wails remained silenced. Soleil placed the broom handle on the trunk and threatened to give it another shake. "Corey," said the Old Ticker. "My name is Corey Willard."

"You wouldn't be lying, would you?" said Flarence.

"It's my name," said the Old Ticker. "It's really my name." Soleil placed the end of the broom handle on his neck and applied pressure, which made the pain flare. "I swear, it's my name. I'm not lying."

"I don't know you," said Gil. "I don't recognize your face or your name. What did my brother and I ever do to you? Does this have something to do with the company we were starting?"

"I don't care who you are or what you do for a living. None of the people I've killed ever did anything to me. None of them were meant to do anything with their lives other than be my breadcrumbs. I needed to leave my mark so I'd know what I'd done, so I'd know what I needed to do. I don't expect any of you to understand."

"We understand completely," said Soleil. "You really are from the future."

"You figured that out by yourselves?" asked the Old Ticker.

"Your magic gun gave it away," said Soleil.

The Old Ticker laughed. "Listen to yourself. You're a grown man describing the gun's abilities as magic. That weapon isn't powered by sorcery."

"We'll get to how it works later," said Soleil. "First, I want to know how many people are using it. Are you alone?" The Old Ticker didn't answer immediately, and Soleil placed the broom handle against the tree again.

"I'm not alone," said the Old Ticker.

"Great," said Soleil. "How many others are there? How many people have guns like these? How many of them traveled back in time with you to this year? Or did they all travel to different points in time?"

"I'm not alone," repeated the Old Ticker.

"I heard you the first time," said Soleil. "Answer the question."

The Old Ticker looked Soleil in the eye. "I'm not alone," he said again.

Soleil whacked the tree, and a berry plopped on the ground near the Old Ticker's ear. It had the shape of a blackberry but was the color of tin. Soleil crushed it with the broom handle. When he lifted it, the tip was stained with dirt and juice. "Oh, that's a good one. The juice has a similar effect as ipecac syrup." The Old Ticker whipped his head back and forth trying to avoid the broom handle, but Soleil got the end into his mouth. He rubbed the handle against his inner cheek, then tossed the broom aside and placed a hand over the Old Ticker's mouth. When the Old Ticker swallowed, Soleil placed one hand on each side of his skull to hold his head still. "Someone hold his legs," he called out. Flarence grabbed his ankles while Claire pinned his shoulders. A moment later, the Old Ticker shook and made gurgling sounds. He convulsed twice, and the third time, a stream of vomit erupted from his mouth and nearly reached Soleil's face. The Old Ticker tried to turn his head to the side but Soleil held it firm, and the vomit in his mouth trickled back down. Soleil let him suffer for a moment before letting go of his head and allowing him to roll over.

FLARENCE

For years, Flarence thought he knew his brother inside and out. Soleil was passive and kind, although somewhat naive. He never stuck his nose in other people's business. He had taken the myth of the Council of Elders to heart and had followed its rules to the letter. As much as Flarence cared about his brother, he always felt Soleil's blind faith made him weak and unable to separate fact from fiction.

His impression had been completely turned around when Soleil pulled that poncho from behind a wall in his cafe and invaded Tymbir's headquarters. Seeing his brother with that broom had changed Flarence's impression again. There was a time when Soleil was just a nobody who owned an unsuccessful cafe. Now he was taking charge, bombarding the shirtless man he had kidnapped with whatever random poisons fell from the branches. For a moment, Flarence was actually afraid that Soleil would go too far and was about to get up and try to calm him down when a voice echoed through the woods.

"Get away from him!"

The voice was unmistakably Darren's. "Told you I wasn't alone," said the Old Ticker. Soleil stood up and looked for Darren, but Flarence and Claire stayed put. They both knew better than to turn their backs on an enemy, even one who appeared weakened. Flarence drew the Stakehail Colt and loaded it. He improved his hearing, but Darren was creating a strong wind which made his position difficult to pinpoint.

"I'm just here to talk," said Darren.

"Oh, now you're ready to talk," said Soleil.

The Old Ticker tried to move, and Claire placed a needle against his throat, forcing him to lie flat on the ground. Flarence also kept the Stakehail Colt aimed at his chest.

"I don't regret what I did," said Darren, "but this is different, and you're not like me. You'll regret what you're doing to the Old Ticker, especially if you kill him. You're upset, and I get it, but what's done is done. Let him go, and this can all be over."

"No, it won't," said Soleil. "You expect me to believe you're here to discuss a truce? You're just here to finish off Gil."

"I don't have any problem with Gil," said Darren.

"It's true," said the Old Ticker. "Gil's mine. And he's wide open."

Flarence was sure it was a bluff. Mohinaux was watching Gil, or at least he was the last time Flarence had checked. Both Gil and Mohinaux were out of Flarence's line of sight, but it was possible that the Old Ticker could see him. Flarence took the bait. "Dad," he called out quietly, but didn't get an answer. "Dad, you've got Gil's back, right? Dad, give me something."

"Shut up, son." Flarence couldn't tell where Mohinaux's voice had come from, but it wasn't where he had been standing with Gil a moment ago. Flarence tore his gaze from the Old Ticker and looked around the clearing but didn't see Gil or Mohinaux anywhere.

Suddenly a blow to the side of the head knocked him over. He heard a yelp, and when he stood up, Claire's face was buried in the branches of the Enchanted tree. The Old Ticker was on his feet with a minor neck wound and a spellcasting revolver in each hand. Darren had deconstructed the fabric strips that bound him.

Though injured, the Old Ticker scampered into the woods. Flarence couldn't bring himself to follow. He pulled Claire away from the tree. Pine needles were stuck in her scarf, but when he pulled it away, he couldn't see any indication the needles had punctured her skin. Whatever was wrong with her must have resulted from inhaling pollen that had fallen behind the scarf. She wasn't moving, and her eyes were unfocused. Flarence shook her and snapped his fingers in front of her eyes, but she didn't respond.

Flarence held Claire close as a fight broke out. Darren had come out of hiding and was darting around frantically to avoid the poisons Soleil threw at him. Mohinaux was closing in on the Old Ticker, who had not been able to run far in his weakened state and was leaning against a nearby tree, firing spells at Mohinaux to keep him at a distance. Flarence thought he could feel Claire's pulse weakening and tried to call to Soleil for help but was drowned out by a war cry from Darren as he hurled his saw blade, which Soleil ducked to avoid. Instead, the blade sailed across the clearing, and struck Mohinaux in the skull.

Mohinaux's head shattered on impact. Fragments of bone and brain burst from his neck and rained around his body as he fell. Everyone froze. When the Old Ticker's laughter broke the silence, Soleil forgot about Darren and ran at him instead. The Old Ticker pressed the switch on his gun a few times, fired at a tree on the other side of the clearing, and then turned the gun on himself. The summoning spell carried him to the tree, and he kept repeating the process, summoning his body deeper into the woods until he was out of sight.

When Soleil turned around, Darren had already reclaimed his blade and disappeared as well. Soleil dropped to his knees near his father's body, staring at him and trying to make sense of what had happened. Flarence was confused as well but more concerned about the friend who was unresponsive in his arms. He called for help but Soleil seemed to be in a trance and stayed next to Mohinaux. Worried and impatient, Flarence shot Soleil in the shoulder to get his attention. "The Old Ticker smashed her head into the tree! What did she get hit with?"

Soleil ran across the clearing and shook Claire by the shoulders as Flarence had a moment ago. He picked up his broom and probed the tree, looking for bent branches and disturbed leaves to indicate where she had been hit. "I think she got some psilocybe sprouts." Flarence saw small, soft nubs in various spots on the tree. "They're small mushrooms," explained Soleil. "They contain a high concentration of the psychedelic compound some species are known for. The compound is in the mushroom itself but it's also excreted, and over time, it forms a film on the surface which dries and flakes off easily. If she ingested it directly, she'd be dead. I'm guessing her scarf protected her mouth and nose, but the compound can also be absorbed through the skin and eyes. If that's what happened, I doubt it will kill her. She couldn't have absorbed a lethal amount. The mushrooms don't look too damaged. Worst case, she'll have a powerful but fleeting high."

Flarence relaxed a little and turned his attention to Mohinaux. "It looks like his head exploded." He walked to the body and examined the shards of tissue that littered the grass, emitting a light steam.

"He was flash frozen," said Soleil. "The Old Ticker must have gotten a head shot with a freeze spell right before Darren hit him with the saw blade."

Flarence couldn't imagine what Soleil was going through. Both of them loved Mohinaux like a father, but Soleil also looked up to him like a hero. "Do we need to take Razor Punk to a hospital?" Flarence asked, partly out of concern for Claire and partially wanting a reason to give Soleil his space.

"It couldn't hurt," said Soleil. "I won't stop you if it makes you feel better. Otherwise, you can take her back to the cafe and keep an eye on her. Do me a favor and take the broom back if you do."

"What are you going to do?"

"I'm taking Dad back to the mountain. He needs to be put to rest somewhere. I'd put him next to Mom, but he never told us where she's buried." Soleil took hold of their father's corpse and disappeared. Flarence lifted Claire and brought her back to Soleil's Cafe.

$$-9-$$

DARREN

Darren had been waiting in the lobby of the burned apartment building for a while, replaying the scene from the forest in his head. Eventually, Dr. Wicker walked in with a new black shirt and a wide smile. "That was incredible!" he shouted as he pumped his hands in the air.

"Did you kill someone and take their shirt?"

Dr. Wicker drew both his guns. "Not this time. I used these to break into a store and stole a shirt." He holstered the guns and traced the chi symbol on his chest. "Now, do me a favor and recreate my markings."

Darren sighed and focused on the dye, which lifted away from the fabric, leaving the white cotton in the form of the appropriate characters. "What did you do to the Student back there?"

"Don't put all the blame on me. We worked together on that one. I froze him to the core and you nailed him with what I must say was an amazing throw."

"You don't know what the Student is capable of. He's going to be pissed when he wakes up."

Dr. Wicker looked at him like he was the dumbest person in the world. "The Student is not going to wake up."

"Genies can heal," said Darren.

"Not from that, they can't. I don't care how powerful you are; if you cut off the head, the body will die, and you did one better by shattering his skull like fine china dropped on a slab of concrete."

Now that Darren thought about it, the chances of healing from a shattered brain seemed farfetched, even for a Genie. A chill ran down his spine. "If the Student is dead, then we just took a piece of Soleil's family away from him. He feels the same way about me as I did about Tymbir."

"So?"

"So we've got to get out of here." Darren grabbed Dr. Wicker and summoned his body away from the apartment building. Their feet touched down on cold pavement. "We're still in Illinois," said Darren as Dr. Wicker looked around, "but Soleil might eventually think to look for me in that apartment building." He noticed Dr. Wicker shivering and warmed the air around them. "Here we have time to talk. It's time you told me how you came up with the names on that list."

Dr. Wicker leaned against the brick wall. "I'm one of the world's leading experts in Chi tech, but even for me, time travel was venturing into uncharted waters. I wasn't sure at first if my experiment was going to work but then realized that if I had gone back in time, it was possible I would have left clues that I was there.

"I started doing some research and noticed little things here and there that weren't immediately eye-catching but still somewhat strange. I came across a surge of autopsies conducted this year in Illinois that all described the cause of death as simply 'unexplained' or 'unusual.'" Dr. Wicker rubbed his hands together. "I dug deeper into the unexplained deaths and found consistencies. People died of frostbite even though they were in a heated home, or burned to death even though there was no evidence of a fire. I figured that must have been me. What really gave it away was a report of the ooze found in the basement of a barn that was owned by Amanda Raik. There's only one weapon that can have that effect on a person."

"But it wasn't all you. I was targeting people on your list as well."

"Not everyone's death exactly matched my gun's capabilities. They were still listed as unusual causes, though, so they were worth checking out. Most of the people in Tymbir's gang died in a hack-slash manner, but the ones found in the field at the university campus seemed to have been killed by Chi tech, and as the victim's families were interviewed, it was discovered that the deceased were part a group which was focused on uncovering crazy urban legends like aliens or supernatural beings. They caught my interest."

"Did you ever consider what you'd do after you were done leaving evidence for your future self?"

"I thought about it when I left, but a lot has taken me by surprise. I thought I was going to do all this alone, but I found that I'm not the only one who can utilize Chi control. I want to know how you're able to use it without the help of a machine."

"Chi control has nothing to do with the spells I cast. What I do is magic, and I don't know how it works. Soleil doesn't know how it works either. Both he and Flarence were born with their powers," said Darren.

"There's no way your mental abilities being so similar to my revolver's capabilities is a coincidence. You even said you have the ability to look into an object's past. I have the ability to travel back in time. We have the same powers. The only difference is that I know how mine work. Don't you want to know how you do what you do?"

"Even if I did, we're in danger. If Soleil isn't willing to let go of his dad's death, and I doubt he will be, you'll never find the answers to any of your questions. You'll be too busy running for your life."

"Why are you so intent on running? I say it's time we stood up for ourselves."

"I killed Tymbir. I don't need to stand up to anyone else, and I don't want any more trouble. I'm starting to think Soleil had the right idea when he preached about staying in the shadows."

"It's too late for that. The trail of bodies left by you and the other Genies is part of what led me to this time period. People have noticed strange things, and investigations are under way. If anything, you're the one being loud, and law enforcement is working in the shadows. It's only a matter of time before someone finds you."

"So what do you recommend?"

"First, let's see if there's anyplace around here that sells bandanas and gloves. I'd like to get the rest of my ensemble back. After that, I say we stop all the secrecy and show Soleil, Flarence, and Razor Punk that we're done playing around."

"We are not going there yet. When I went off the deep end, Soleil tried reasoning with me even when he had the chance to kill me. I owe him the same courtesy."

"If your impressions of Soleil are accurate, he's likely to lose his temper the second he sees you. There's only one place we know he's going to check out that requires him to stay calm."

The two headed for the nearest clothing store.

SOLEIL

Mohinaux's body lay unburied on the floor of the cave. Soleil knew he should say something to honor his father's memory but hadn't been able to speak a single sentence without breaking into tears. He just sat against a boulder sobbing. When Flarence appeared, he swallowed hard and dried his eyes. "Is Claire back on her feet?" he asked.

"She's coming down," said Flarence as he moved the dirt near Mohinaux to form a grave. "She's still groggy. I gave her some water. I also gave her the Stakehail Colt in case she needs to protect herself, but I still don't want to leave her alone for long."

"You could have brought her with you."

The grave looked deep enough but Flarence didn't push the body in just yet. "She didn't want to come. He's our dad, but Claire mainly knew him as the Student. He tried to hurt her. I can't blame her for not having a lot of nice things to say about him."

Soleil found the strength to stand up and approach Mohinaux's body. "Maybe she'd have something nice to say if you'd brought her over once in a while. If she's like family to you, the least you could've done was introduce her to your father."

"Dad and I never really got along. He was always telling me to find a master, reinforcing the importance of following the rules, and going on about the Council of Elders."

"In hindsight, I guess it was a stupid story, but I trusted him," said Soleil. "I never had the urge to question him the way you did. I always took him to be the wise old man with all the answers. I wanted to believe I could turn to him whenever I needed help." Soleil knelt down and held Mohinaux's shoulders while Flarence grabbed his ankles, and the two dropped him into the grave. "I also wanted him to be around forever. For humans, that's too much to ask, but I believed that for people like us, it might've actually been a possibility."

Flarence moved the pile of dirt into the hole. "What are you going to do now? I know you didn't want to kill Darren before. Does this change things?"

"Of course this changes things," said Soleil. "If I had exterminated Darren earlier, this wouldn't have happened. The way I see it, killing Darren, the Old Ticker, and Inspector R.E.D. is a way to honor Dad's memory."

Flarence sighed with relief, knowing that he and his brother were finally on the same page. "Come to think of it, Inspector R.E.D. wasn't in the forest earlier. I wonder if he's still working with the others."

"He might have been there and we were too preoccupied to notice. If he was hiding in the trees, he would've seen Gil run off when the fight broke out."

"If he'd stuck around long enough, he might have seen me carrying Claire back to your cafe after she was drugged," said Flarence.

They summoned their bodies to the cafe, landing in Soleil's bedroom simultaneously to find Claire at the edge of the bed. Her palms rested against the frame and held her upper body a few inches above it while her legs extended straight out. Her arms and legs were shaking, and her face cringed as she tried to hold her position. When she saw Soleil and Flarence, her arms relaxed and she fell back onto the mattress. "I'm not one hundred percent yet," she said as Flarence went downstairs to make sure they were alone. "I'm feeling better, though. I'll be back on my feet in no time."

Soleil brought her a glass of water. "You should be resting," he said.

"Sleeping things off makes me feel lazy," said Claire as she scooted to the backrest and gulped the water. "I feel better when my blood is pumping faster. Why do you two look worried?"

"We're just concerned about you," Flarence said when he came back, lying on the bed with his head perpendicular to Claire's feet. "I'll be right back." He closed his eyes and his body went limp.

Claire drained the glass and put it back on the bedside table. "The first time I found him projecting in bed, I freaked out and slapped him until my palms were numb trying to wake him up," she said. Soleil smiled. "The second time, I drew on his face in permanent marker. He raided a drug dealer's hideout wearing a goatee and devil horns." Again, Soleil said nothing. She was about to mention the third time when Flarence sat up.

"Wow," he said. "We fucked up royal on this one!"

"Gil's dead?" asked Soleil.

"See for yourself," said Flarence.

Soleil sat on the floor with his back on the wall. His projection found Gil's body floating down the Des Plaines River. Roy must have carried Gil away from the clearing and killed him, then dumped his body in the water. Gil's death had clearly been much slower and more painful than Roy's other victims. There were the characteristic bullet holes in his chest but in addition his face had been badly beaten. His eyes had been gouged out, his nose was broken, his lips were swollen, and it looked like patches of his hair had been torn out by hand. It also looked like Roy had ripped his limbs part-way off. His arms and legs were bent at improper angles and Soleil thought that Gil's chest looked misshapen as well, as if every one of his ribs had been broken. His projection returned to his body, and he counted all the people he hadn't been able to save. Not just Tymbir and Gil but also Tymbir's friends who were murdered by Darren and the Old Ticker, along with Gil's business partners. Worst of all, his own father, his headless body buried in a mountain.

"We tried our best," said Claire after Flarence described Gil's condition to her. "Maybe this is over. Now that Tymbir and Gil are dead, everyone's gotten their revenge."

"This isn't over," said Soleil. "They can't just commit multiple murders and then go on as if nothing happened."

"I'm with you," said Flarence, "but the Old Ticker lied about his name. I tried sending a projection to him while looking after Claire but couldn't get a fix on him. We have no way of finding him."

"We'll come up with a plan later when we're all feeling better," said Soleil. "Claire is right. Now that Tymbir and Gil are dead, Darren and Inspector R.E.D. will probably calm down. We can't let them get away with what they've done, but at least we have some time to breathe." He stood up and left the room. "I'm getting something to eat—do you want anything?"

Flarence wanted a sandwich, and Claire wanted a burger. Soleil made a plate of pasta with meat sauce and a side of garlic bread for himself, and when he was finished, he created a hole in the ceiling and floated the plates into his room. They hovered in the air for a few moments before Flarence called out, "Got 'em!"

Soleil stayed downstairs, preferring to be alone. As he ate, he couldn't stop replaying the images of his father's head exploding and Tymbir's being slashed in the cave. He didn't have strong feelings for Gil but still felt sick after seeing the beaten and deformed body floating in the river. He shoveled the food into his mouth faster, hoping the garlic and tomatoes would push the images out of his mind, but the memories continued even as he scraped his plate clean. When eating his problems away failed, Soleil tried focusing on something positive. He reminded himself that Roy had gotten Emma away from danger before finishing off Gil. She was the only still-living person he had tried to keep safe. Soleil decided he should check on her.

When his projection approached Emma's hospital, he saw people inside screaming and trampling each other to run out the doors. Emma was still in a bed on the third floor, and while the screaming was audible there, the danger seemed concentrated in the lobby. Some people who heard the noise were rushing to the stairs; others were demanding to know what was happening.

It didn't take Soleil's projection long to find the source of the lobby commotion. Standing on the front desk was the Old Ticker, wearing a new shirt and mask emblazoned with his usual symbols and firing his guns. The security personnel and people behind the front desk were dead. Soleil was sure that Darren was somewhere in the mess as well.

FLARENCE

Neither Flarence nor Clare was in a mood to talk; the only sounds were their chewing as they sat side-by-side on the bed. Soleil had made a chicken sandwich piled with cheese, lettuce, tomatoes, onions, and a generous helping of his homemade ranch dressing, so the dish was more of a handheld salad than a sandwich. The dressing and the juices from the tomatoes and chicken dripped down Flarence's hand, and he raced to lick the streams before they stained his sleeves. Claire's burger also had lots of vegetables, and the meat, cooked rare, was dripping with juice and homemade hot sauce, which Flarence knew from experience had a serious kick. As Claire ate, her nose ran, and she was constantly taking breaks from scarfing down the burger to rub the back of her hand under her nose. It was terrible table manners, but they weren't at a table, and they were both comfortable enough with each other to be gross once in a while. Flarence belched loudly, and Claire snorted deeply to keep the mucus from running down her upper lip.

Flarence had two bites left of his sandwich when Soleil leaped up through the floor. "We need to go!" he shouted. "Darren and the

Old Ticker are attacking a hospital. I think they're going after Emma." Before Flarence could say anything, Soleil grabbed him by the shoulders, and he dropped his plate on the floor near Emma's hospital bed. She was asleep, surrounded by machines. The door was closed, but outside, he could hear people running and shouting.

Soleil started to disconnect the devices, but Flarence grabbed his wrist. "What do you think you're doing? We can't just grab her and run; moving her might hurt her more. Let's focus on the people we know how to handle. I'll go back and get Razor Punk."

"Fine, I won't move Emma," said Soleil, "but Razor Punk isn't fully recovered. She said so herself, and the Old Ticker is going crazy with his spellcasting revolvers in the lobby. If we're going to stop him, we need to get down there now." Soleil and Flarence ran to the stairs, since, with so many people moving around below, falling through the floor risked landing on top of someone. Many people had escaped, and others were following shelter-in-place procedures, so the stairwell was mostly empty.

Among the few people on the stairs, they saw Darren. When he saw Soleil and Flarence, he put his foot on the handrail and pushed off, removing his saw blade as he glided up several levels. Soleil and Flarence also made their bodies weightless and pursued him.

They all stopped on a high, unoccupied floor. "I don't suppose you're still willing to talk," said Darren. Soleil removed a vial from his poncho and popped the cork off. Before he could throw it, Darren manipulated the air around him to create a protective cyclone. "I didn't think so. Just so you know—killing your father wasn't part of the plan." He spread his arms, gesturing to the hospital building. "None of this was part of the plan, but I'm glad it happened. You understand what I went through now. What you're feeling is exactly what I felt when Atalissa died. This is what you wanted me to move on from. You wanted me to forgive Tymbir for what he did. Can you forgive me for what I did?"

Soleil responded by throwing the vial, which was deflected by the wind.

"I'll handle him," said Flarence as he drew the Stakehail Colt. "Get to the lobby. I'm sure the Old Ticker is still down there wreaking havoc. Besides, it's going to take more than an indoor twister to block my weapons." Soleil seemed reluctant but complied.

"I'm not a hypocrite for wanting to kill you now," said Flarence after Soleil had left. "I never trusted you in the first place."

"Yeah? Well, I never liked you," said Darren as the wind swirled more violently, "and I'm pretty sure I can make a breeze strong enough to deflect your icicles."

The twister around Darren became so strong that it nearly knocked Flarence back. He had no doubt the force was indeed strong enough to deflect his icicles, so instead, he deconstructed the floor under Darren's feet and leaped off the railing. Darren, not anticipating this, fell through the hole, crumpling as he hit the platform below. Flarence hovered his body in the air as he fired the Stakehail Colt.

Darren recovered more quickly than Flarence had hoped, and rolled away as he regained his footing. Five shots missed, but the sixth hit Darren in the shoulder. Flarence opened the gun, but before he could reload, Darren tore the icicle out of his shoulder and lunged at Flarence, swinging the saw blade as he flew. Flarence, with no time to reload, threw a punch with the Wrist Cannon. The doorknob and blade collided, and the impact sent both men's bodies flying in different directions. Flarence grabbed a railing and launched himself at his foe, who did the same. Again, there was a clang as the doorknob struck the saw and sent both men on new trajectories. Again and again, they soared at one another like lancers in a zero gravity joust until Darren caught hold of Flarence's wrist. The two spun for a moment and then Flarence felt his body falling. Darren had restored his body's weight and was dragging them both down the center of the stairwell, straight to the ground floor.

Flarence turned all his focus to the moisture in the air and loaded the Stakehail Colt, then closed it by slapping the cylinder and gas tank against Darren's chest. He pressed the barrel below Darren's ribs, and fired as many times as he could before their impact with the ground—

three shots before he felt like every bone in his body was shattered. He had landed on his back after a ten-story drop, with Darren on top of him. He couldn't move and his whole body was tingling.

Bit by bit, Flarence regained control. He started wiggling his toes, then bent his knees. When he finally could sit up, he saw that he was alone in the stairwell. Even though Darren's fall had been cushioned somewhat by Flarence's body, it had likely left him in bad shape and forced him to summon-travel someplace he could be alone and heal.

Flarence decided being alone was his best option too, and summoned his body back to the cafe. Soleil was sitting at a table with Claire. She was moving the dial on the portable radio back and forth while Soleil was examining his left hand, which had some light bruising on the palm and wrist. He also had a nosebleed. "What happened to you?" asked Flarence.

"The Old Ticker hit me in the hand with a shock spell while I was holding a vial of a blood thinner," said Soleil. "The shock made my muscles contract, and I broke it. Some of the liquid seeped into the wounds before I healed. I'll be fine in a little bit." He wiped his nose on his sleeve. "I didn't want to risk getting injured while the blood thinner's effects were still getting to me, so I came back here. What happened to you?"

Flarence didn't want to get into details. "I got my ass kicked," he said.

"There," said Claire as she put the radio down on the table, "I finally found a station that comes in clear." Flarence took a seat and listened to a weather report, a traffic update, and an interview with a photojournalist whose work was going to be exhibited at the Art Institute of Chicago. "What station is this?" asked Claire. "There's a massacre at a hospital, and these people are talking to some loser who spent a year telling strangers to smile and say cheese."

"I know you're impatient, but show some respect," said Soleil. "Art matters." After a few minutes, the interview was interrupted by another reporter saying, "This just in . . . ."

"Finally," muttered Claire as the reporter went on to describe the events at the hospital, calling it a possible hostage situation although no one knew how many people were being held captive. Witnesses who had gotten away told the reporter they'd heard screaming and had run, but a few who'd been in the lobby described a masked man jumping on the front desk with a strange gun. Some described a wide range of injuries to the victims, from severe burns to people who were liquefied. The first witnesses interviewed described the events as supernatural, then the word paranormal was thrown around a few times, and finally the word magic was used. Soleil groaned and slouched in his chair.

"Nobody who hears this is going to take any of those testimonies seriously," said Flarence. "Everyone is going to assume the people were traumatized and seeing crazy things."

"Maybe at first, but it's not going to last," said Soleil. "If the reporters stay there, eventually, someone's going to get footage of the Old Ticker using his gun."

"This also isn't the first time Darren's used his powers in public," said Claire. "Or you, for that matter," she added, looking at Flarence.

"Well, if they're going to be open with their powers, we might as well do the same," he replied.

Soleil stood up. "You're right. From now on, there's no holding back. Claire, how are you feeling?"

"Better," she said, "but sit down. Running in there without a plan is why you and Flarence got beat up. Let's work something out before we go back."

$$-10-$$

DARREN

"Another one," said Dr. Wicker as he placed the barrel of his gun against the temple of a doctor who had not escaped. The man whimpered as he set up a bag and slid a needle into Darren's arm to collect another sample of Enchanted blood. Five other prisoners were sitting with their backs against the wall on the opposite side of the room. There were people on other floors, but Darren and Dr. Wicker decided to keep an eye on only a handful of them.

"You're scaring him," said Darren. "At least put the gun away."

"I don't think so," said Dr. Wicker. "This is a standoff situation. There are cops outside, and we have hostages. If we start acting nice, people aren't going to take us seriously. We already let one of them go. That's the only kind act I'm performing today." Darren had taken the cell phone of the man they released and ordered him to tell police the number, and that if they did not receive a call within the hour, a hostage would be killed.

The second bag of blood was full, and the terrified resident removed the needle. He was about to set up for another collection when Darren pushed him against the wall with the other prisoners. Darren and Dr. Wicker each collected one of the blood bags and stood outside the room. "Nobody's going to take us seriously anyway if we don't have a reason for what we're doing," said Darren. "This wasn't the plan. We were supposed to go to Emma's room and wait for Soleil to show up so I could convince him to leave me alone.

Fighting was our last resort. You definitely weren't supposed to jump up on the front desk and get all trigger happy."

"The plan was to gain a deeper understanding of your powers." Dr. Wicker held the bag close to his face and shook it. "I need control of this hospital to analyze these samples and find out what makes you tick."

"Fine, but if this is a standoff situation, what exactly are our demands?"

Dr. Wicker shrugged. "We'll just make something up to buy time. You can leave that part to me if you want."

The released hostage's phone rang, and Dr. Wicker walked down the hall as he answered it. Darren returned to where the hostages were, his saw blade out and ready to strike if Soleil or Flarence appeared. Emma was still in her bed, but he didn't need her anymore to lure Soleil to the hospital, so he didn't see a point in watching her. Darren approached a hostage and read the information on his laminated badge. "You there, nurse Doug, can you analyze this?"

Doug immediately nodded but then looked confused. "Analyze it for what?"

Darren pulled him to his feet. "Anything you know how to do, I guess. If you try to get away, we'll know, and we'll kill you before you reach the front door."

The man scurried down the hall as Dr. Wicker returned. "You're not going to believe this," he said as he put the cell phone in his pocket. "The guy I talked to is named Broadsord. I knew my old boss's family had history in the armed forces and public services, but I never imagined it went back this far. I must have been speaking with one of General Broadsord's distant relatives. This means we need to be careful before attacking the cops. If the Broadsord bloodline ends here, I might never be hired by the military. As for our demands, I told them we want $2 million."

"Actually, I do want $2 million," said Darren.

"I'm sure you do," said Dr. Wicker, "but I doubt they'll actually give it to us, so let's focus on the task at hand. I'm very interested in observing what effects your blood might have on various species. We've already seen what being injected with Enchanted blood can do to a human corpse. Inspector R.E.D. is gone, but maybe he can be replaced."

Before Dr. Wicker could give any details of his plan, Darren heard a sound in a nearby room. "Get your gun out. We're not alone."

A door opened and a barrage of surgical tools bombarded Darren and Dr. Wicker. Darren instinctively tried to deconstruct them but wasn't quick enough to get them all. Dr. Wicker yelped as two scalpels struck his arm. Darren helped him remove them, and when he looked up, he saw the sole of a shoe. The impact knocked him down, and he slid a few feet on the floor. When he stood up, Claire was pummeling and slashing Dr. Wicker with a razor blade. She knocked one of his guns out of his hands and kicked it away. Dr. Wicker tried to shoot her but missed and deconstructed a section of a wall, which Claire ran through before Darren could throw his saw blade at her. Dr. Wicker retrieved his gun, and the two men followed her.

The room they went into had only two shelves on a wall and no place to hide. Dr. Wicker walked toward an open door on the other side of the room, but Darren stopped him. "What's wrong?" said Dr. Wicker impatiently.

"She's holding back," said Darren. "It's not like her to hit and run." Dr. Wicker took a moment to register what Darren had said. His eyes widened as he pieced the facts together, and the two men ran back to their holding room. All the hostages were gone.

SOLEIL

The nurse Soleil had taken from the holding room backed away from Emma's bed. "Is it okay to move her?" Soleil whispered.

The nurse nodded. "She'll be fine, but I would strongly recommend getting her to another hospital. Can you heal her?"

"The short answer is no." He held the nurse's wrist and wrapped his other arm around Emma, then summoned his body to a police car outside the hospital where Flarence had brought the other hostages. The officers were confused but quickly adapting to the situation. When Soleil appeared, someone took Emma to an ambulance. Soon after it left, Flarence appeared with Claire.

"We got most of them," said Flarence, "but there are still some people confined to their beds. It's going to be tough to save everyone."

A man in uniform approached them. "Somebody better explain to me what's going on."

"These three just appeared out of thin air, sir," said another officer.

"I saw that part. I also noticed that they appeared with some of the hostages."

Soleil slowly extended his arm. "My name's Soleil. I take it you're in charge here."

The man didn't shake Soleil's hand. "You're right." He looked at Flarence's right arm and took in Claire's attire. "There's something familiar about you two."

"You've probably heard someone mention us," said Flarence. "We tend to get involved in criminal activities from time to time. She's Razor Punk and I'm Glacial Lightning."

Soleil punched Flarence in the shoulder. "Stop saying that."

"I've heard stories," said Broadsord. "I always took you for urban legends."

"We're real," said Flarence, "and we're here to help. If nothing else, you need to understand what you're up against."

"I know exactly what I'm dealing with," said Broadsord. "Backup is on the way, and I'm sure we'll be able to bring them down without further loss of life."

"No, you won't," said Soleil. "The Old Ticker has a weapon that casts spells, and bullets aren't going to do a thing against his partner. Whatever you're planning, you need to call it off."

"Which one of you is named Broadsord?" Soleil recognized Darren's voice, magically amplified so it sounded like he was speaking through a megaphone, but didn't see him anywhere.

"He's invisible," said Soleil. "Everybody shut up." He improved his hearing and listened for anything that would give away Darren's location.

The man in charge puffed his chest. "I'm Jethro Broadsord. Who am I speaking to?"

"You idiot!" shouted Claire. Darren was visible just long enough for Soleil to see him grab Broadsord and disappear.

FLARENCE

As soon as Darren disappeared, the police car next to Flarence lurched across the parking area toward a larger truck. He and Claire sidestepped to avoid it, but several officers didn't react in time and were mowed down. As the car collided with the truck, Darren reappeared and ran through the crowd of officers. As hard as he was hitting them, they were protected by their body armor against most of the blows. Darren's swing was at a bad angle, and the jagged edge of his saw blade got caught in one man's thick vest. The officer wrestled Darren to the ground and pinned him, then yelped as his body was lifted off Darren and flown to a building across the street. Darren leaped back to his feet and summoned the blade to his body. He continued assaulting the police, focusing on where the armor didn't protect them.

Flarence looked up and saw the Old Ticker standing in a window with his guns drawn, sending a rain of spells down on them. For a moment, Flarence considered deconstructing the part of the building where the Old Ticker was standing but remembered there were still people in the hospital who'd been too sick to flee. If he triggered a collapse, some of them would be hurt or killed. A better option would be to shoot the Old Ticker, but he was outside the gas-powered Stakehail Colt's effective lethal range.

Flarence ran to a trio of officers who had their guns out and were shooting at Darren. He pointed to the window where the Old

Ticker was standing. "There! Shoot that one!" The officers looked to where Flarence was pointing and started firing at the masked man. It didn't look like he was hit, but the Old Ticker retreated. Flarence saw Soleil close by with a vial in each hand, looking unsure of what to do. "Get to the Old Ticker," Flarence instructed. "Force him back to the window and give these guys a shot at him. We'll handle things down here." Soleil nodded and disappeared.

Flarence pulled out his Stakehail Colt and loaded it. "Keep your eyes on that window," he told the officers. "Razor Punk and I will watch your back. When you see the masked man again, shoot him down." Scanning the area, Flarence spotted Darren nearby struggling with an officer who had him in a chokehold. Darren increased his weight as he dropped to his knees, pulling the officer with him, then flipped her over his shoulder. When she hit the ground, her hold loosened, and Darren cut her face. She screamed and held her hand over an eye as blood flowed through her fingers but stopped when he kicked her in the neck. Then Darren saw Flarence and the three officers and ran at them. Flarence fired the Stakehail Colt twice, but his shots were deflected with two swings of the saw blade. Flarence hesitated, waiting for Darren to get closer to fire again.

But before he could, Claire leaped from behind a police car and knocked Darren down with a drop kick. She hit him a few times while he was down, then had to leap away to avoid being cut. As soon as Darren stood up, Flarence fired four icicles into his chest. As he removed them, Claire delivered a punch to the head that knocked him down again.

The sound of gunfire erupted behind Flarence from the three officers firing at the Old Ticker. Darren tried to get to them, but Claire and Flarence kept him at a distance. Suddenly Darren disappeared. Flarence and Claire spun around to see where he had summoned his body. Then they heard a scream and looked up at the hospital to see Soleil falling. The Old Ticker was still in the window but now standing behind Darren. Soleil's descent slowed until he was suspended in midair. The Old Ticker pushed past Darren and fired a spell that took Soleil's focus off the gravity manipulation and started him falling again. As soon as he hit the pavement, Darren grabbed the Old Ticker by the wrist, and in an instant, they were gone.

Flarence and Claire ran to Soleil, who had part of a broken leg sticking out through his skin. Flarence put away the Stakehail Colt as Claire straightened Soleil's bone and held it in place so it could heal properly.

"Do you think they're still in the hospital?" asked Flarence.

"Let's find out," said Claire as Soleil stood up.

"We should wait for backup to get here," said one of the remaining officers.

"When they get here, tell them all to stay back," said Soleil. "You saw what those two are capable of. You're not equipped to handle this."

One of the officers looked at Flarence. "You told us to shoot the guy in the mask."

"Guns will work on him," said Flarence, "but not on the other guy."

"Then we'll take care of half the problem," said an officer.

—11—

DARREN

Nurse Doug prepared the equipment at gunpoint. Dr. Wicker held a cup of water as Darren lay in an MRI machine. There was a specific series of procedures Dr. Wicker wanted to take Darren through to examine how his body operated, but they needed to work quickly to get as much information as possible before Soleil, Flarence, Claire, and the police succeeded in driving them out. In another room, samples of blood from the two bags were spinning in a centrifuge. In the hallway sat another cup filled with Enchanted blood as well as a splash of soda from the cafeteria to make it smell sweet.

"All right, we have an image on the screen," Dr. Wicker called. "We're ready when you are." Darren focused on the cup of water and caused it to freeze, then melt, then boil. It reminded him of the days in his old apartment when he first acquired powers and spent hours practicing by casting spells on whatever was laying around. After a few cycles of temperature manipulation, Dr. Wicker told him that was enough. When the bed slid out and the MRI machine was turned off, Darren asked Dr. Wicker what, if anything, he had learned.

"We'll talk while we walk," said Dr. Wicker as he moved toward the door and motioned for Darren to follow. Nurse Doug stood up but Dr. Wicker held out his hand. "We don't need you for anything else at the moment. If we have another purpose, we'll find you. If you run, we'll shoot you down."

Dr. Wicker left the room and Darren followed close behind, neither caring whether their prisoner stayed or fled. "When you first went into the machine, your brain displayed normal activity," Dr. Wicker explained as they made their way down the hall, "but once you started casting spells, certain sections started to light up."

They reached the room with the centrifuge. Dr. Wicker lifted the lid and removed the vials, one with Darren's Enchanted blood and the other with Dr. Wicker's normal blood. They looked similar, but the one labeled with Darren's name had an extra layer of fluid. "The gunk at the bottom is your cells," said Dr. Wicker. "They sink because they're the heaviest component in the solution. The liquid above that is your plasma. Both of those things are normal. It's this part that catches my attention." He pointed to the thick film floating on top. It had a slight blue fluorescence. "If that's what I think it is, there's no need to be alarmed by its presence. Everyone has it in them. Just nowhere near this volume." In the distance, they could hear quick footsteps. "It sounds like our hostage decided to run."

Darren placed a finger over his lips and improved his hearing. "He's not the only one out there. I can hear more footsteps down the hall. Get your guns out."

SOLEIL

The three of them crept down the hallway as quietly as possible, hoping that Darren wasn't using his super hearing ability. They found Nurse Doug, who told them that Darren and the Old Ticker were experimenting with blood samples, and directed them to the room with the centrifuge. Some of the machines in the room were big enough to hide behind. "Do you think they're in here?" asked Flarence.

Soleil removed a vial of powder from his poncho, uncorked it, and slid it across the floor. He backed out of the room, motioned for Flarence and Claire to follow him, and closed the door. "I'll circulate the air in there and get the poison to disperse," said Soleil. "At the very least, it'll flush them out."

Suddenly the door turned to dust and Darren's flying saw blade hit Soleil's shoulder. He tried to take it out, but before he could touch it, the blade flew back to Darren, who caught it and leaped up through the ceiling. Soleil followed, and as soon as his feet touched the ground, the blade flew his way again.

This time, Soleil was prepared and dodged it. He took out another vial and controlled the air to create a cyclone that sucked out the contents and directed them down the hall. Darren leaped up through the ceiling again to avoid the cloud of poison. Soleil deconstructed the section of ceiling where Darren had jumped and created a vacuum that sucked the poison onto the floor above, but was interrupted when another hole appeared directly above his head and Darren fell through it, landing right behind him. Soleil avoided the swing of the saw blade, but a kick to the back sent him sprawling across the floor. Instead of advancing, Darren retreated several steps.

"You almost killed me in the field because I let you get too close," said Darren. "I'm not making that mistake again." He darted to his left and passed through a wall.

It appeared that Darren was going to be fighting from a distance from now on. Soleil wished he had taken the time to construct a ranged weapon like Flarence's Stakehail Colt, or at least bought a regular gun and learned how to use it. He followed Darren into the next room, but as soon as he entered, he had to jump to avoid the flying saw blade. Before he could attack, Darren had passed through another wall. Soleil looked around the room for something useful, and noticed a bottle of isopropyl alcohol. He picked it up, made the bottle invisible, and ran into the hallway.

He poked his head out of the room slowly, ready to retreat if Darren was outside waiting for him, but found the hallway empty. He improved his hearing to get a sense of where Darren had gone. The sounds of footsteps were drowned out by a buzzing noise. He followed the noise and after a few turns found Darren, who was entranced and didn't see Soleil approaching. Soleil was about to strike when he spotted what had caught Darren's attention. At the end of the hall, a Styrofoam cup was under a window, and the remnants of fluid were being sucked up by a creature that took Soleil a moment to recognize. It was the size of a fully-grown Rottweiler, but it had an exoskeleton and more than four legs. When it turned and faced Soleil, its eyes gave away its identity. As if Darren and the Old Ticker weren't trouble enough, an Enchanted fly was now loose in the hospital.

FLARENCE

With both his guns back, the Old Ticker was hard to pin down. Every icicle Flarence shot was melted by the heat spell, and every time Claire got close, the Old Ticker shot himself with a summoning spell that sent his body to a wall on the opposite side of the room, then fired an attacking spell with the other gun.

The Old Ticker was getting tired, and his panting made his mask wave back and forth. Claire was tiring and slowing down too. Flarence, trying to end the fight quickly before she collapsed from exhaustion, became more aggressive. He ignored the pain of the Old Ticker's spells and tried to get close enough to land a hit but had not been able to do any damage. He was so lost in the fury of battle that he didn't notice Darren run into the room with Soleil behind him. It wasn't until he felt a rush of wind by his ear that he realized there was another monster to worry about. The Enchanted fly darted around the room madly, trying to knock someone to the ground. Flarence tried to ignore it and focus on the Old Ticker.

Then Claire screamed. He turned and saw her on the ground with the fly on top spewing a thick fluid onto her leg. Flarence aimed the Stakehail Colt, but before he could shoot, Soleil threw a plastic bottle at the creature. The plastic fell apart, and the fly was showered with a clear liquid. It leaped off Claire and hovered for a moment before the fluid burst into flames. Shocked, frightened, and in pain, the Enchanted fly whizzed around the room, buzzing louder and crashing into the walls and ceiling.

Flarence pocketed the Stakehail Colt and ran to Claire, who was in tears as she clutched her leg. The fabric of her jeans was dissolving, and the chains under it were falling apart. Holding her close, he summoned his body to their hotel, then summoned the liquefied fabric to the walls of the room. Not all the fluid had reached her skin, but what touched her flesh brought welts and gashes.

Flarence knew she needed help, but before he could focus on any-place near a hospital, Soleil appeared, grabbed them both, and performed a summoning spell. Flarence figured he would have gone back to his cafe, but when his feet touched solid ground, the place was unfamiliar. He was about to ask where he was, but Soleil was already banging on a door. When it opened, Soleil reached inside and wheeled someone out of the room.

"Darren won't attack if he sees Tyrell with us," said Soleil. "He won't put his son in danger. At least I hope he won't." The four of them stayed still for a moment, Claire moaning through clenched teeth.

After a minute passed, Tyrell broke the silence. "Whatever happened, it looks like she needs to go to a hospital."

"If she does, one of us will have to stay close to her at all times," said Flarence.

"Even if we took her to a hospital, the doctors might not be able to help," said Soleil. "She'd heal faster if she had powers."

"Don't you dare," said Claire.

"We don't know what we're dealing with," said Soleil. "Beelzebub just tried to pre-digest your leg. That fluid was likely different than a typical fly's juices, and it could have lasting effects."

"What can we expect?" said Flarence. "Was an Enchanted fly ever mentioned in Dad's journal?"

"Yes, but this was different," said Soleil. "It didn't look exactly like the creature Dad described. I think it changed because it drank some of Darren's blood, but it wasn't fully Enchanted."

"Then it's not as bad as it could have been," Claire hissed through clenched teeth. "Just give it some time. I can't stand right now, but I'll rest and keep it clean as possible."

"If it doesn't get better, I'm giving you healing powers," said Soleil.

"Soleil, if you Enchant me, I swear I'll spend every second of my eternal life kicking your ass."

"It's her choice," said Flarence. "Besides, you said that she's safe here."

"He said she's safe as long as I'm here," said Tyrell. "He's right that Dad won't try anything if there's a chance of me getting hurt, but I can't be around all the time. I'm only staying in this townhouse temporarily, and while I can skip a few classes, eventually people will notice and come by to check on me."

"I don't intend on letting this drag on that long," said Flarence. He formed a block of ice in his hand. Tyrell wrapped it in a few squares of paper towels and held it on Claire's leg as Flarence and Soleil caught him up on everything that had happened.

"This is going to end tonight if I have anything to say about it," said Flarence. "Soleil and I will bring you and Claire to a doctor, and then we're going right back to finish off the Old Ticker and Darren. Don't leave her side while we're gone."

"Finish him off?" said Tyrell. "Soleil, you're still not going to kill Dad, right?"

Soleil placed his hands on Tyrell's wheelchair. "Where's the nearest hospital?" he said, dodging the question

—12—

DARREN

"You just had to stomp on it, didn't you," said Dr. Wicker as he and Darren once again waited for the centrifuge to stop spinning. "That specimen would have been much more interesting to study alive." After the flaming Enchanted fly crashed into a wall and fell to the floor, Darren had thoroughly crushed it. Once it was dead, he performed an astral projection to find Claire, who Dr. Wicker insisted they finish off, but he refused to attack in Tyrell's home.

"That specimen was a threat to everyone, including us," said Darren. He gestured to the centrifuge. "Besides, it looks like you're still getting some use out of it."

The centrifuge stopped whirring, and Dr. Wicker lifted the lid. The Enchanted fly's blood looked different from Darren's but the same bluish substance was present. "You want to tell me what that is now?" asked Darren.

"It's something that will cause quite a stir in a few years," said Dr. Wicker. He raised the test tube and tilted it to make the light bounce off the fluid. "I never studied it myself, but I've followed other people's work closely. This field of research has been going on for some time in one way or another. I'm sure you're somewhat familiar with some processes that deal with linking hallucinogenic drugs with spiritual experiences. Have you ever heard of peyote?"

Darren slapped his palm against his forehead. "You're telling me Genies naturally produce drugs? That's what makes us magic?"

"Not exactly," said Dr. Wicker. "That's only one compound that was used and studied. Later came the discovery of DMT, also known as the Spirit Molecule. It's a chemical humans produce naturally in small quantities, but when test subjects were given a large dose, they experienced what some considered visions."

He lowered the vial and walked in circles around the centrifuge, gesturing as he spoke. "Research into the Spirit Molecule was replaced when a new substance was discovered, informally known as Liquid Soul. Humans also produce it naturally in small quantities. When the dose was increased, it amplified the effects of other biologic substances, particularly hormones. A solution of adrenaline and Liquid Soul made subjects much more energetic than adrenaline alone in the control groups. In fact, it gave some people bursts of superhuman strength and stamina. Applying Liquid Soul to norepinephrine made subjects highly alert and focused. It was mixing Liquid Soul with melatonin which caught the attention of people interested in metaphysics. Melatonin is a hormone which regulates sleep cycles."

"So, what—did it put people in comas?" said Darren.

Dr. Wicker stopped pacing. He placed the test tube back in the centrifuge and spun the holder with his hand. "It's what happened while they were in their coma that was interesting. Everyone who received treatment was able to recall their dreams vividly, and some were convinced that they were actually glimpses into the afterlife. Others thought they had seen the future. Results of Liquid Soul experiments became famous. There were movies about it as well as blogs, songs, and rallies to increase funding for more studies. Naturally, there was resistance as well. Many people believed that Liquid Soul fanatics were drug addicts looking to score a free high."

"Some of them probably were," said Darren, "but did any of the people in the Liquid Soul experiments gain abilities like mine?"

Dr. Wicker caressed the gun in his holster. "Nobody became like you, but I think that's because they were missing a key component. I believe that your powers are the result of an interaction between

Chi boson activity and Liquid Soul production. Chi bosons are generated from the Chi field, which can't be felt but is present everywhere in this world and across the universe. Stimulating Chi field activity in close proximity with living cells may produce a positive feedback response, where exposure to the boson activity increases Liquid Soul production, and that production further expands a person's connection with the Chi field. If that's the case, it emphasizes my point about why the Student can't have recovered. Liquid Soul is produced in the brain. That's a Genie's weak point."

Darren tapped his temple. "I've been shot in the head before. It didn't stop me."

Dr. Wicker held his thumb and index finger close together. "I'm talking about a gland approximately this big. It would take a very precise shot to destroy it. Or if that's too difficult, pulverize the brain altogether." He waved his hands around. "But that's beside the point. If this is true, it's a remarkable discovery. I studied Chi bosons because I hoped that an understanding of how the universe could be controlled would one day lead to a deeper understanding of how it was created. Liquid Soul provided a possible way to study the human spirit. I hoped that one day I would find a link between the two."

"Its weird hearing you get spiritual considering all the people you've killed for your research."

Dr. Wicker crossed his arms. "Yes, in my attempt to find God, I've condemned my soul. The irony is not lost on me. But spiritual status and deities aside, it seems my efforts have been rewarded. I thought I had unlocked the key to controlling the most powerful force in the universe, but I now see that my revolvers are a glass half-full, as were Inspector R.E.D. and the fly.

"My gun controls Chi bosons, and the fly consumed a highly concentrated solution of Liquid Soul. But in your case, both those things happen simultaneously. Somehow, the compound and the field are interacting with one another and giving you powers that my guns can't match. Not only are you able to control forces but your body is nearly indestructible. Furthermore, you're able to share the power. What you did to Inspector R.E.D. shows that you can reanimate the dead. I want to try and take it a step farther."

"We can't go any further than raising the dead," said Darren.

Dr. Wicker spun the centrifuge one more time and then approached Darren. He drew a gun with one hand and pointed to his head with the other. "I bet we can. Like I said, small amounts of Liquid Soul are produced naturally in a specific gland in the human brain. Animals also have this gland. If I'm right in thinking that Chi bosons and Liquid Soul have a synergistic effect on each other, it's possible that exposure to a Chi boson source could stimulate Liquid Soul production."

Darren wasn't sure he understood everything that was said but couldn't think of any questions that would help him make sense of it, so he followed quietly to the Enchanted fly. Dr. Wicker severed the wings and put them under his arm as the two went to leave. Darren heard footfalls in the distance. He held up his hand, signaling Dr. Wicker to stop moving. He improved his hearing and listened to a group of people at the end of the hallway, along with the static of a radio and a soft voice whispering their location. "The cavalry has arrived," said Darren.

Dr. Wicker dropped the wings and reached for his second gun. Before he could get it out of the holster, both sides of the hallway erupted with gunfire. Darren deconstructed the bullets as Dr. Wicker fired spells to both ends of the hall. The gunfire ended, but so many bullets had been fired that the resulting metal dust clouded their vision. Darren increased the weight of the particulates, and as soon as the cloud settled, the team of officers was nearly on them.

This group was packing more heat than the officers he had faced in the parking lot earlier; they were armed with enormous rifles and large metal shields, which were glowing from the heat spell Dr. Wicker had fired. To make matters worse, Soleil and Flarence were with them. Darren first turned the agents' guns to dust, then their shields. As soon as he did, they all drew other firearms, but Darren's deconstruction spell was quicker.

Giving up on engaging in a firefight, the team charged. Darren deconstructed their Kevlar vests, some of which were instantly re-formed by Soleil or Flarence. Darren swung his saw blade at the agents' throats but was taking hits as often as he was delivering them. Then he saw more people with guns, body armor, and shields making their way down the hall. The group he had disarmed was only the first wave, and now reinforcements were closing in. Darren disarmed them too, though it drew his attention from the fight in front of him, and he took a few more blows. Darren's healing power gave him enough of an edge to hold his ground, but Dr. Wicker was not faring as well. He fired spells as fast as he could, but Flarence and some officers were closing in. Darren tried to help but his feet suddenly gave out and he was flat on the floor. He rolled over and saw Soleil standing over him holding a vial.

Darren held his breath, but before Soleil could remove the cork, there was a red and white blur, and Soleil was gone. Darren sat up and saw that Flarence was not near Dr. Wicker anymore. Both of them lay sprawled at opposite sides of the hallway, and standing among the agents was Roy. His mask and lab coat were torn, and he wasn't wearing his gloves anymore, but his powers still seemed to be intact. He moved quickly—too fast for Darren's eyes to follow—as he pummeled the officers. Some of the reinforcements ran, but most stayed and fought, as did Soleil and Flarence. Roy dealt with the attackers by crushing their throats, ripping their arms off, and sending the bullets in his chest their way. Flarence had a handful of icicles, but Darren melted them and lunged at him before he could make more. As they fought, Dr. Wicker crawled away.

Flarence landed a blow to Darren's jaw with the Wrist Cannon, and Darren slashed Flarence's forehead. Neither of them were doing any lasting damage, but then Roy charged past Darren and grabbed Flarence's arm. The bones snapped and Flarence screamed but quickly pivoted to be in a position for his arm to heal. As soon as it did, Roy broke the arm in a different place before throwing him to the floor. Flarence got up and delivered a punch with the Wrist

Cannon. Roy blocked it and repeated the continual bone breaking. When Roy let go again, Flarence disappeared, apparently having had enough of the pain.

Darren looked around and saw that Soleil was also gone. "Thanks," he said. "Where have you been?"

Roy looked back and forth from Darren to Dr. Wicker, who was sitting against a wall holding his side and coughing. As good as he was with his guns, he wasn't much of a fighter. "I needed some time to think," said Roy.

There was a beeping noise, and Darren turned to see an officer on the floor with a walkie-talkie near his mouth. Blood was streaming down his head, and he looked shaken. "Sir," he said in a weak voice, "anyone listening. Something . . . inhuman here. Strong. Fast. Smells like death. Skin . . . clammy, decaying. I think it's . . . a zombie." Roy knelt over the wounded officer, wrenched away the walkie-talkie, and broke both it and the man's neck.

"It's good to have you back," said Dr. Wicker who slowly made his way to his dropped guns. "Darren and I will fill you in on our recent discoveries, but we need to make it quick. There might be another attack soon, so I would like to collect the necessary components as quickly as possible."

SOLEIL

Jethro Broadsord, who had made his way back after being carried several miles from the hospital by Darren's summoning spell, sat in the front seat of a police car with Flarence and Soleil in back. He set his walkie-talkie on the dashboard and looked at them in the rearview mirror. "Did I hear that right? My people were attacked by a zombie?"

"He's not a zombie," said Soleil. "He's an Enchanted corpse. Darren reanimated him with a blood transfusion. We're still not sure exactly how it works."

"We were able to kill him once by injecting him with water," said Flarence, "but it was tough. He's fast and strong, and even after we killed him, he was just brought back to life again."

"So you're saying there are three of them and two of you," said Broadsord. "And you've already explained that guns and armor are useless with Darren around. We need to focus on our advantages. Water kills the Enchanted corpse. Are there any other weaknesses we can exploit?"

"The Old Ticker's nothing without his guns," said Flarence. "He can't heal and he doesn't have enhanced strength or senses. If we can get him alone and disarm him, we can kill him quickly."

"The only way to kill Darren is to obliterate his brain," said Soleil. "At least, that's how he killed our father."

"It's back!" a nearby voice called. Outside the car, Roy was beating people and throwing them around. Broadsord stepped out of the car and drew his gun. Soleil and Flarence followed. Roy was next to Broadsord in seconds, wrenched the gun out of his hand, bent it, and threw it away. Then he grabbed Broadsord by the shoulders and pinned him against the police car.

"I'm not here to hurt anyone this time," said Roy. "Just play along. Darren might be watching us." He let go of Broadsord and punched Soleil in the face. "I don't trust Dr. Wicker."

Flarence struck Roy in the temple with the Wrist Cannon. "Who?"

"The Old Ticker," said Roy. "His name is Dr. Emmanuel Wicker. There's something he's not telling us, and I don't think he and Darren ended up here by accident. He knows the area too well."

Soleil took a vial from his poncho, and Roy batted it out of his hand. "What do you mean he knows the area?" said Soleil.

Roy threw Soleil against the car and kicked Flarence in the chest. "There's a building nearby. It's a biological research facility. Dr. Wicker told Darren to summon him there while I created a distraction out here. It seems like a weird plan, and it doesn't sit right with me."

"Punch me in the face," said Flarence. Roy complied and Flarence fell to the ground and rolled under the car. "You and Soleil keep fighting," he called out. "I'll keep an eye on Dr. Wicker."

FLARENCE

From under the car, Flarence performed an astral projection and found Dr. Wicker with Darren in a building near the hospital. The room they were in had dozens of cages, each with a monkey screaming and beating on the bars. Dr. Wicker's right hand held a dog's severed head, while his left dragged a dead rat by the tail. The rat was larger than it should have been, and Flarence guessed it had been Enchanted before being killed.

Darren opened a cage, then caught the Rhesus monkey inside as it tried to escape. Its terrified screams intensified as Darren summoned a few of its teeth to a nearby wall. The monkey growled and transformed into a Sasquatch. Its size and strength became too much to control, and Darren hacked at the monster's head until the growling stopped and the creature was motionless, killed in mid-Enchantment. Flarence noticed that the rat had a head wound as well. Darren grabbed a handful of the Sasquatch's fur in one hand and Dr. Wicker's arm in the other, and they disappeared. Flarence's projection returned to his body, and he rolled out from under the car.

"They're collecting dead monsters," he said as he head-butted Roy. "Any idea what the bodies are for?"

Roy threw him to the ground. "It's got something to do with re-animation. Run but don't go far. You know the Old Ticker's name now, so you can spy on him. Get somewhere safe and use astral projections to keep an eye on us. I'll try to get more information."

The three traded blows to continue their illusion of fighting, then Soleil and Flarence summoned their bodies to the cafe.

"Do you trust him?" asked Soleil.

"Not a chance," said Flarence. "I'll project. You stay alert in case one of them shows up unexpectedly."

—13—

DARREN

Darren was not comfortable killing the animals, especially the dog, which had been killed without its being Enchanted, but at least he learned something from it that he could use against Soleil and Flarence. Before going to the biological research facility, Dr. Wicker had drawn a diagram of a brain and highlighted a small section that he said was responsible for producing Liquid Soul. He reasoned that if both Liquid Soul and Chi bosons were needed for magical powers, then removing the gland would render the Enchanted animals powerless and therefore killable.

Darren hadn't exactly removed the glands but had hacked at the animals' skulls until his saw blade was stained with brain matter. Keeping the blade in the space where the gland that produced Liquid Soul was presumed to be prevented it from reforming. Since the animals stopped changing, he figured the hunch was correct.

He was glad to have confirmed a Genie's weak point but would feel more comfortable if he had an idea of what Dr. Wicker was planning. While he called himself a doctor, he clearly had no medical experience. He amputated body parts with medical instruments he had found, but his cutting was sloppy. Blood spilled out of the Enchanted animals, and as Dr. Wicker whipped a surgical bone saw back and forth, fluids splattered on the walls. Once the body parts were removed, he organized them into piles: one for limbs, another for tails, another for abdomens, and another for heads. He had also salvaged several parts of the fly.

When all the animals were cut up and their parts sorted, Dr. Wicker took a step back to take in his work. He inhaled deeply, savoring the smell of death the same way Darren had savored the feeling after killing Tymbir. After a moment of silence, Dr. Wicker looked like a man possessed. His eyes became focused and he dove into one of the piles. He removed the torso of the Sasquatch and brought it to the bed of the MRI machine. Then he rushed back to another pile and took the rat's tail, which had grown to about five feet long. He mashed the tail where the monkey's arm had been and with one of his guns burned the tissue hot enough for the two parts to meld together. Darren went over to the head pile and picked up what remained of one of the fly's eyes.

"No!" said Dr. Wicker. "Please, don't touch anything. Allow me. I know what I'm doing."

"How?" Roy asked, as Dr. Wicker retrieved the dog's leg and held it against the Sasquatch's other shoulder. Dr. Wicker walked back to the pile of body parts, but Roy stopped him. "I asked you a question. How do you know what you're doing?"

"Calm down," said Darren.

"He's using us," said Roy. "I don't know what for, but it seems like he's too familiar with what's been going on. He chose to attack this place because it's close to the biological research facility, and he killed those specific animals for a reason. There's some kind of higher purpose to all of this."

"You're right," said Dr. Wicker, "there is a higher purpose, but there's no need to be nervous. We will all benefit from it. After tonight, you won't have to worry about Soleil or Flarence anymore."

"What happens tonight?" asked Darren.

"Something Earth-shattering," said Dr. Wicker.

"Nothing's going to happen tonight," said Roy. "You're going to die before you have the chance to perform any more of your experiments."

Before Roy could make a move, Darren grabbed hold of his sleeve and pulled him back. Roy turned and raised a fist but hesitated and lowered it.

"Fine. If you don't want me to kill him, I won't, but you have to admit this has gone too far. It started with the two of us holding a grudge against a few people. Now we're taking over hospitals. I'm done. Whatever Earth-shattering thing Dr. Wicker thinks we're going to cause isn't happening. I'm not some rat in his cage." Roy started walking out of the room, but before he could leave, Dr. Wicker drew his gun and fired. Roy screamed and fell to the floor.

"You have every right to refuse if that's what you want," said Dr. Wicker, "but if you're not with me, you're against me, and if you're against me, you're too powerful to live." Roy tried to stand up but couldn't hold his footing and fell on his stomach. "There's more than one way to rupture cells," said Dr. Wicker. "Freezing causes the water inside them to expand and break." Roy writhed on the floor as he had when Flarence killed him at the barn.

SOLEIL

Flarence jolted as he regained consciousness. "Inspector R.E.D. is down. Also, he was right. The Old Ticker is preparing something."

"When you say he's down, do you mean he's dead again?" asked Soleil.

"It looks like it. If we can get to him, we can revive him. It would be nice having him on our side." Flarence grabbed Soleil's wrist and summoned their bodies to a hallway in the hospital. In a nearby room, Darren and Dr. Wicker were shouting at each other. Soleil tapped his ears, indicating he wanted Flarence to improve his hearing. Then he became invisible and crept into the room. Flarence stayed ready to back up his brother if another fight broke out.

"All he did was ask a question," said Darren.

Soleil entered the room and saw Darren near Roy's limp body and Dr. Wicker standing on the other side of the room in a pool of blood surrounded by rotting flesh and meat. Soleil crept toward Roy as the two continued their conversation.

"He turned against us, and I would rather not have him as an enemy," said Dr. Wicker.

"We could have talked him back on our side," said Darren. "Now that you killed him, he's definitely not going to be with us, even if I bring him back."

"We don't need him anymore," said Dr. Wicker. "When this works—and it will—there will be a new monster on our side, one superior to Inspector R.E.D. in every . . . ."

"Shut up," interrupted Darren. There was a moment's hesitation, then he swung his foot. Darren's foot stopped in midair as Soleil grabbed it and became visible. He tripped Darren and ran to Roy, but Dr. Wicker caught him with an electrocution spell. The pain made him stumble and miss Roy. Flarence stood at the doorway and fired several icicles at Dr. Wicker.

"Hold them off," Soleil called as he ran to Roy. Their hands met, and Soleil summoned them to a car in the parking lot. Hoping some residual power still resonated in the corpse, he shook and slapped Roy. It had no effect. He needed Enchanted blood, and needed it fast. Soleil didn't have a syringe, and any cut would heal too quickly to be useful.

Soleil lifted Roy's shirt. He selected a vial of purple liquid, hesitated before flicking off the cork, and cringed as he gulped it down. Then he shattered the end of the vial and drove it into Roy like a stake. In a moment, the poison took effect, and a stream of blood erupted from Soleil's mouth. Much of it splashed about uncontrollably, but some flowed through the glass tube into Roy's body.

The taste was terrible, and there was an intense pain in his stomach, but Soleil maintained his position and directed the blood into Roy as best he could. The purging eased momentarily, letting Soleil remove the tube and impale Roy closer to his heart. He wasn't sure it mattered but assumed having multiple entry points was better. Soon, the heaving ceased, and Soleil leaned back against the destroyed car as he waited for Roy to come back from death for a third time.

FLARENCE

"Darren landed a cheap shot," said Flarence, who appeared at a nearby lamp post with a gash on his neck and ran to Soleil. "What did you do?"

"I don't want to talk about it," said Soleil.

They both stood over Roy, waiting for him to show any signs of life. "How many liquid poisons do you have left?"

Soleil pulled several vials out of his poncho. "This one is like a highly concentrated solution of capsaicin. It won't slow Darren down much, but if we can force it down the Old Ticker's throat, it'll take him out. This one is what I used against Darren in the field that almost killed him. It's metabolized into carbon monoxide and will asphyxiate him. This one is an acid which erodes tooth enamel like you wouldn't believe. When animals ingested this one, it caused breathing problems followed by impaired muscle coordination, paralysis, and then death. I don't know if all those things would happen to Darren."

"Does the last one have to be swallowed?"

"I don't know. The only route of entry I tried when testing it on squirrels was dousing food with it."

"Give it to me," said Flarence. Soleil handed him the vial and he put it in the inner pocket of his jacket. "I just hope Roy gets back on his feet soon."

—14—

DARREN

Dr. Wicker panted like he had just completed a marathon as he made the final adjustments to the creature on the MRI table. The dog's head was loosely attached to what remained of the Sasquatch's neck, and a hole in its skull exposed part of its brain. Pieces of a disassembled spellcasting revolver were strewn about the room, and Dr. Wicker held up a device that seemed to radiate some kind of energy. "This is the source of Chi bosons," he explained as he brought the device to the creature. "I'm going to implant it close to the gland that produces Liquid Soul. The two will interact and give it access to the Chi field."

"You're sure that will work?" said Darren.

"I'm positive," said Dr. Wicker as he placed the device on the creature's brain tissue. Then he picked up the chunk of skull bone he had removed and mashed it in place. Once the skull fragment was secure enough not to fall off, he started the MRI machine as he had seen Doug do, causing the bed to move into the chamber. They went to look at the monitor, although Darren had no idea what he was supposed to be looking for.

"You never answered Inspector R.E.D.'s question," said Darren. "You said something big is going to happen."

"That's how I know this is going to work. There really was a monster on the loose that day. Sorry, I mean today. I can't believe I assumed this was entirely my work. Knowing what I know now, even I have to laugh at my arrogance." Dr. Wicker pointed to the computer screen where a tiny yellow-green dot appeared on what had been a gray silhouette of the creature's brain. "It's happening!" Dr. Wicker shouted as he bounced on the balls of his feet.

Darren placed a hand on Dr. Wicker's shoulder and forced him to be still. "What's happening?"

"I wasn't entirely honest with you before. I did have a hypothesis regarding the time-traveling application of Chi bosons, and I did have a feeling that if it worked, I would end up in this time period, but the unexplained murders weren't my only clues. I was confident I would arrive here because this was the year an event occurred. In my time, it's referred to as the Anomaly. I was one of many people fascinated with it and spent countless hours trying to find an explanation. Of course, I wasn't born until years after it happened. The city was rebuilt, so my only resources were recorded testimonies of survivors."

"Wait, the city had to be rebuilt?" said Darren. "What happened?"

"Buildings crumbled, streets were destroyed, thousands of people died, and several natural disasters occurred simultaneously. It's been said there was a twister, a hurricane, and the world's largest recorded hail. It all happened and ended abruptly. Many thought it was the end of the world, and some who lived through it claimed they saw a monster in the midst of the destruction. Some were even able to describe the monster in detail.

"The Anomaly has been studied from many angles. People have reviewed weather patterns, but there was nothing abnormal prior to the event. Geologists believe an earthquake knocked down the buildings, but records don't show seismic activity of the necessary magnitude. As my studies progressed, I realized that Chi tech could have caused some of the events that were described, but I had no explanation as to who could have been using it. Once I delved into the possibility of time travel, I entertained the radical idea that I was the one in control. I caused the Anomaly."

"Why didn't you tell me this before?"

"Chi tech could have caused some of the events but not all of them. Even if my time traveling experiment worked, there were things my guns wouldn't be able to do. I met you and the other Genies and realized that I wasn't the only one responsible. You're going to help me cause the Anomaly. At least, you are now. I was worried that if I told you earlier that the plan was to destroy the city, you wouldn't have wanted any part of it."

Darren's grip tightened on his saw blade. "Inspector R.E.D. was right. You've been using us."

"I'm sorry I didn't tell you everything, but I've been trying to help you. All this time you've been holding back. Every time we've fought, it's been in a cave, or a secluded farmhouse. This war is no longer a secret. I made a scene at the hospital today for this very reason. I'm pushing you to take the fight to the streets and let the world know what you're capable of. I don't know how you Genies got your powers, but I know that you're very difficult to kill. If you keep holding back, the fighting will never end. It's time to let loose. Bring a building down on Flarence's head. Use something bigger than your saw blade. You know his weakness now. Aim for the gland. The violence won't end until only one of you is left, and the only way to make that happen is to go after Flarence and Soleil with everything you've got."

"Do I survive the Anomaly?" said Darren. "Do Flarence or Soleil survive?"

"If Flarence or Soleil survived, don't you think they would have tried to stop me before I traveled back in time?" said Dr. Wicker.

"I thought doctors were supposed to be smart," said Darren. "If they stopped you, it would create a paradox. If you never traveled back in time, the Anomaly would never have happened, which means they'd have no reason to stop you from traveling back in time."

"You're not listening," said Dr. Wicker. "My original hypothesis was that I caused the Anomaly, but that doesn't appear to be the case at all. I didn't kill all those people. I didn't destroy the city. It was you. If I never went back in time, the Anomaly would still happen, just in a different way. You, Flarence, and Soleil have been heading for a showdown for a while. I'm just along for the ride. It's been humbling, discovering that I'm actually not at the center of it all, but at the end of the day, I'm just glad I discovered the true cause."

Darren pinned Dr. Wicker against a wall. "I'm glad you found the answer to your question. Now answer mine: Am I alive in the future?"

Dr. Wicker pulled on Darren's wrists. "I don't know," he admitted after failing to break free. "I never heard of you until I traveled back in time."

"So you're saying I don't make it."

"I don't know that for sure. All I can say is you and I never make contact in the future. I never heard of Soleil or Flarence until I traveled back in time either. It's possible that I'm the one who doesn't make it while you simply disappear after killing those two."

There was a thud, and they looked at the MRI machine to see the creature's limbs undergoing violent spasms. The computer screen was now brightly lit with multiple colors. The creature was growing. The rat tail that had been attached to its shoulder now extended past the creature's feet, and while it was flexible, the flesh was transforming. "Are those scales?" asked Darren.

"The fact that it can move means the body parts are aligning and joining together," said Dr. Wicker. "The different kinds of tissues are combining as well. The rat tail is merging with the fly's exoskeleton. It's growing pretty fast. We should probably get it out before it gets stuck."

Dr. Wicker pressed a button and the table slid out of the MRI machine. The creature rolled off and squirmed on the floor, making sounds that Darren could only describe as something between a shriek and a howl. The wings on its back expanded and fluttered, which made it flop as if it was throwing a tantrum. He and Dr. Wicker stood quietly and watched as their monster continued to grow and change. After a few minutes of thrashing, the monster lay on its back, so still Darren wasn't sure it was breathing. "Is it dead?" he asked.

"It can't be," said Dr. Wicker. "This is the monster the survivors of the Anomaly said they saw. I'm sure of it. It will revive in a moment. It has to."

SOLEIL

The blood had taken effect and Roy was back on his feet, telling them about the things that had happened at the hospital. He didn't have a firm grasp on all of it, and Soleil was having a hard time making sense of everything he was hearing, but it seemed that Dr. Wicker had discovered the source of magic.

"We're not retreating this time," said Soleil as they faced the main entrance. "The more he discovers, the more dangerous he becomes. We need to kill him this time—at any cost."

Darren and Dr. Wicker greeted them at the entrance, standing with their hands linked. Neither of them moved as Soleil and Flarence drew their weapons.

"Darren, think about this," said Roy. "You've put innocent people in danger. You've hurt people who haven't done anything wrong. That's not what this was about." Soleil couldn't believe it. The man he once considered a monster was trying to reason with the enemy, making one final attempt at a non-violent solution. Roy had a heart after all, even if it was riddled with bullets.

"Of course that's what this was about," said Darren. "Tymbir wasn't my only enemy. I was victimized long before I met him. People have been shooting at me since before we met."

"Being shot will feel like a scrape soon," said Dr. Wicker. "Things are going to get a lot worse before they get better."

"What does that mean?" asked Flarence.

"It means I'm from the future," said Dr. Wicker. "I know what happens next, and it doesn't look good for you."

"You're not his puppet," said Roy. "Whatever he told you, you don't have to do it."

"I know I don't have to," said Darren. "I'm doing this because I want to. I'm sick of being a beggar and a whipping boy. That's not me anymore. I used to be a small fish in a big pond. Now I'm Poseidon."

Flarence turned his attention to Dr. Wicker. "What did you tell him?" he shouted. "What happens next?"

"That should be obvious," said Dr. Wicker. "We fight."

Roy attacked first. He leaped toward the doors, covering the distance in one jump. But Darren's summoning spell was faster, and Roy punched air as Darren and Dr. Wicker moved to a nearby lamp post. Flarence fired his Stakehail Colt in their direction, but Dr. Wicker melted the icicle with a heat spell. Soleil threw a dart, which was crushed by a cluster of falling bricks. He figured Darren had deconstructed part of the hospital to make it rain down on them, but then he heard a snarl behind him. He turned and faced the most hideous creature he had ever seen.

Its torso looked like a human's with toned abdominal and chest muscles. Its right arm looked like a bear's: large and strong and reaching almost to its knees, covered with fur and ending in thick claws. The left arm was completely different. Instead of fur, it was scaled and much longer than the right, extending to the creature's feet, where it rolled into a coil like a snake. Instead of claws, there was what appeared to be a stinger at the tip.

The creature's legs were equal in length, covered in fur, and ending with what resembled a rat's paws. The head was furry with pointed ears and a snout like a wolf's, but directly above its dark nose was a protruding structure that looked like a fleshy straw. The teeth were not canines but instead looked like a shark's. Each one was razor sharp, and there were two rows of them. On the creature's back was a pair of thin wings like an insect's. "There it is," cried Dr. Wicker, "the greatest scientific achievement to date. Humans have finally created life. A one-of-a-kind species. I call it the Bionuclear Beast!"

Soleil knew it by another name. It was the first entry he had seen in Mohinaux's journal. "Flarence," he muttered, "that's the Cannibal."

For a moment, all Soleil could do was stand still as the creature's head darted back and forth, looking at each of them. Soleil wondered what the Cannibal was thinking, assuming it was even capable of rational thought. Was it in pain? Was it frightened? It wasn't attacking anyone yet; did that mean it was docile? Perhaps it considered the hospital its territory, and if everyone left, it would go back inside, curl up, and go to sleep.

Soleil's train of thought was interrupted when Flarence screamed as he was hit by a heat spell. The Cannibal seemed to be shocked by the sudden loud noise. It howled and leaped forward, beating its wings madly to move, and headed for Flarence. Soleil dove and met it in midair. They hit the concrete, the Cannibal still howling and thrashing. Soleil did his best to hold on to the monster, but it was strong and flailing wildly. The Cannibal thrust its clawed arm at Soleil's neck, but Roy stopped it before it ripped his throat open. The struggle continued, but the Cannibal was too strong to pin down even with Roy and Soleil working together. Suddenly Soleil felt a sharp pain in his arm as the Cannibal locked its jaws around his bicep. He struggled to break free but stopped when he heard the intense buzzing and realized he was off the ground. The Cannibal was carrying him away from the fight.

FLARENCE

Darren and Dr. Wicker were still holding hands, and every time Roy ran at them, Darren performed a summoning spell to move out of his grasp. Flarence tried to shoot them but also was too slow, and none of his shots hit their targets. Darren and Dr. Wicker were making no attempt to fight back and were entirely focused on evasive tactics. Their game of tag went on until Flarence realized that Darren was laughing.

"That's enough of that," said Darren, disappearing and then reappearing by the hospital doors. "It's time I did my part." He let go of Dr. Wicker's hand and vanished. Dr. Wicker turned his gun and fired a summoning spell at his head, then extended his arm and fired at a distant object.

A series of explosions echoed east of the hospital while screams erupted in the west. "I'll follow the fire," said Flarence. "You follow the screams." Neither of them hesitated. Roy bolted down the street, while Flarence floated up until he was high enough to see a trail of flames lining a distant street, and summoned his body to a spot near the destruction. He arrived in front of Darren, who was standing in the middle of the road with his arms spread wide.

As he walked, the lines of parked cars on both sides of him erupted, one after the other. Flarence realized Darren was heating the gasoline in the tanks to make them explode. As soon as Flarence arrived, the explosions stopped. Darren stood in a fighting stance and raised his saw blade. Flarence raised his weapons as well, the Wrist Cannon level with his chin and the Stakehail Colt aimed at Darren's throat.

—15—

DARREN

Dr. Wicker was right when he said the Anomaly was inevitable. If he and Flarence continued their course, neither would get anywhere. This time it was for keeps. This time Darren wasn't going to attack with just the saw blade. The city was his weapon.

Darren summoned his body to a flaming mid-sized sedan, reduced its weight, and picked it up by the front bumper. With one hand, he swung it like a club. Flarence backed away to avoid the blow. Darren advanced on Flarence again, but when he tried to swing the car once more, it turned to dust in his hand.

Then Flarence fired an icicle, which Darren deflected with his saw blade before focusing on the pile of debris around his feet. Instead of recreating the car, he molded the metal and plastic into a lance and charged at Flarence, who once again deconstructed the weapon. Now that Darren was close, Flarence could grapple with him. Darren tried to struggle free, but their legs got tangled. The two fell to the street, wrestling on the ground.

Darren continued to struggle physically while focusing mentally on the smoking cars around him. He deconstructed all the cars he had blown up and reconstructed them into hundreds of orbs approximately sixteen inches in diameter. Then he made the orbs weightless so they rose up, blew about in the wind, and then crashed to the ground when Darren restored their weight. Both Darren and Flarence were hit, making Flarence let go. Darren stood up, lunged, and swung his blade, cutting deep into Flarence's forearm. Flarence shouted and drove his shoulder into Darren's chest, sending him staggering backward and tripping on one of the orbs.

When Darren stood up, the metal orbs were floating again, hovering a few feet above the ground, some level with Darren's knees and others with his eyes. Flarence punched one of them with his Wrist Cannon, sending it forward like a billiard ball to collide with another, which in turn collided with another. Darren's eyes darted around as he tried to follow the trail and ducked to narrowly avoid an orb flying at his head, and then nearly fell when an orb hit the back of his leg.

The metallic clanking of the colliding orbs became louder, and Darren realized Flarence was jabbing away at multiple orbs, each punch resulting in a new chain reaction. Deciding two could play that game, Darren directed some of the chaos toward Flarence by swinging his saw blade at a few nearby orbs. The collisions quickly became so violent and rapid that Darren lost his sense of direction. He spun, ducked, and staggered as he tried to avoid being struck, and lashed out with his saw blade every chance he had. Dodging all the orbs was impossible, and Darren was being pummeled without knowing if any of his attacks were hitting Flarence. While the hits he was taking were not life-threatening, being in the cloud of floating metal was making him dizzy, which made him vulnerable. Darren made his body weightless and leaped up to escape, hovering above the spheres as the collisions continued.

There, he found Flarence, who was also weightless and floating. Darren manipulated the air to create a jet stream that pushed his body toward his foe. Flarence did likewise. The two collided and grabbed each other, grappling and punching as they floated above the street. Darren broke Flarence's hold and threw him through the window of the nearest building. Then he deconstructed its base, making the building teeter and crumble with Flarence inside. The building smashed into a larger one, which also fell apart.

The two structures kicked up a cloud of dust as they toppled, and Darren drifted upward to avoid being enveloped. When the crashing ceased, he increased his weight and drifted slowly down to the wreckage, creating a twister around his body to blow the dust away. When his feet touched the ground, he searched through the debris. Bodies were littered throughout the rubble, some of them still alive and moaning. He grabbed the nearest injured person and examined his face. It wasn't Flarence. He let the body drop and looked at another, searching the wreckage as fast as he could, hoping Flarence was injured and pinned so he could deliver a killing blow.

SOLEIL

Screams were coming from every direction, and Soleil knew he should be helping, but he needed to wait for his torn Achilles tendon to heal. The Cannibal was strong, fast, and bloodthirsty, but it was also unfocused, which gave Soleil the time to heal. It wasn't hunting for food or protecting its territory but simply lashing out against everyone within striking distance, not caring if the wounds it inflicted were superficial, crippling, or fatal. The moment Soleil hit the ground, the Cannibal leaped on someone else nearby.

As grateful as Soleil was that his head had not been torn off, he feared he wasn't going to be able to find a way to kill the monster. He had been trying to give it a dose of poison, but the Cannibal's wings enabled it to move quickly, even though it couldn't fly long distances, so that when Soleil prepared to lob a vial, the monster darted between buildings like a grasshopper in a field.

As Soleil sat on a curb waiting for his leg to heal, he recalled what Mohinaux had told him and realized he might not be able to kill the Cannibal. Was this the same creature that Mohinaux had fought in the desert eons ago? He had never shown Darren his father's journal or told him about the Cannibal, and yet he was now facing an exact replica of that monster, along with a man who could travel through time. It couldn't be a coincidence. Somehow the Cannibal was going to be sent into the past. Soleil just hoped that he was the one who would find a way to do it, and that it wouldn't cost him his life.

The throbbing in his leg subsided and he rose to his feet, ready for another round. He thought he had become numb to the screaming, but when he faced the Cannibal, what he saw made him pause. The monster's teeth were locked onto a young woman's neck, while its snake-like arm was crushing an elderly man. As the two struggled, a middle-aged man armed with a baseball bat ran to help, but the Cannibal struck out with its other arm, embedding its claws deep into the man's stomach and lifting him several inches off the ground. Once the woman stopped struggling, the Cannibal bit down hard, and she fell to the ground with half her neck missing. The old man stopped moving soon afterward and was thrown into a nearby car while the third man was dropped, still alive.

The Cannibal knelt over him, placed its head above his stomach and inserted the appendage that looked like a straw into the gaping wound. Soleil realized that what extended from the Cannibal's snout was the fly's proboscis, which had grown to many times its normal size. The man screamed as the same fluid that had rendered Claire immobile dissolved his organs before the Cannibal drove its snout into the hole and greedily lapped the man's softened innards.

Soleil attacked, hoping to catch the Cannibal off guard as it drank. But the monster, sensing him coming, lifted its foot and caught him in the chest. It knelt down, and Soleil threw his hand up, grabbing the creature by the neck and holding it back as its teeth gnashed inches away from his face. With his other hand, Soleil drove a dart into the Cannibal's chest. The monster's thick muscles kept the dart from going in very deep, but the pain made it jump off Soleil. The poison seemed to have no immediate effect, and Soleil, not knowing the Cannibal's metabolism, wasn't sure it would do anything at all. But he couldn't wait around to find out. The only way to keep the creature's victims to a minimum was to keep it focused on one person.

Soleil attacked again. The Cannibal swatted at him with its clawed arm, and he bobbed to avoid it. He pulled a vial of powder out of his poncho, but when he opened it, the Cannibal flapped its wings and flew away, creating a gust that sent the powder drifting toward Soleil. He held his breath and summoned his body to a nearby building to escape the poisonous dust. Then he saw the Cannibal crouched on top of a street lamp and was about to attack it again but was pulled away. When he looked up, Roy was standing next to him, and a smoldering car was resting upside down where he'd been a moment ago. Dr. Wicker was standing half a block away with his gun pointed in their direction.

"When he saw you, he lit a car on fire and summoned it your direction," said Roy. "He's not easy to take down."

"Neither is the Cannibal," said Soleil. "I don't want to try to take on both the doctor and his creation at the same time. We need to put some distance between us."

Roy bolted to the street lamp and punched its base to make it collapse. The Cannibal leaped to the next lamp post, which Roy also brought down. He was about to repeat the process again but was interrupted by a distant rumbling, which spooked the Cannibal and caused it to retreat. In the distance, a building toppled into another, sending a massive dust cloud their way. Soleil knew that either Flarence or Darren had done it. Dr. Wicker turned the gun to his head, preparing a summoning spell. Soleil decided that escaping was a good option for everyone and turned to tell Roy but found that he was already gone.

FLARENCE

He was probably the only one to make it out of the building before it fell. As soon as he was thrown through the window, he sensed Darren's intentions and summoned his body to a minivan a few blocks away. A cloud of dust enveloped him, and he had to create a gale to keep the particles away from his face. Once things calmed down, Flarence crept through the cloud toward the demolished building. All around him people were crying and screaming, which made improved hearing useless as a detection method. He blew the dust away from his face and looked closely through the haze.

Soon he was walking through more than just dust. He nearly tripped over a pile of bricks and cut his suit on steel posts and metal pipes. Keeping the Stakehail Colt extended, he took a deep breath and shouted into the cloud. "Darren, you were right when you said you're not a whipping boy anymore, but you're still a loser as far as I'm concerned." He waited for Darren to respond and reveal his location. There was no reply.

Flarence continued taunting. "Even with all your powers, you're just a low-life. The only way you can feel good about yourself is by proving you're strong, and the only way you can feel strong is by hurting others. You're pathetic." Darren still did not take the bait.

"Soleil once described you as a family man," Flarence continued. "I don't know how he got that idea. You're a lazy, selfish deadbeat. Your death was the best thing to ever happen to Atalissa. While you were hanging out with your friends and coming to terms with life in the slums, Tyrell was working hard trying to get out. The only thing you did right as a father was push your son away."

Bringing up Tyrell was Darren's red button, and Flarence hit it hard. The air around him suddenly became very warm, and a strong wind cleared the dust in an instant. With the cover gone, he could see Darren clearly, standing on top of a pile of bricks. Flarence ran toward him to get close enough for the Stakehail Colt to be useful. He couldn't risk missing the next time he fired. Darren stood his ground but the wind was getting stronger and making Flarence lose his footing. He felt his feet leave the ground as a tornado formed. Darren, standing in the eye of the storm, was affected less. The gas-powered Stakehail Colt was useless, and there was no object near Darren large enough to summon his body to.

Flarence tried manipulating the temperature to stop the tornado from forming, but a sharp pain in his foot broke his concentration. He looked down and saw a metal pipe embedded in his ankle. He wrenched it out, but as soon as he did, a brick hit his side. The tornado became too powerful, and Flarence was lifted into the air. Being tossed about in the wind and pummeled by debris was disorienting, but in the confusion, he saw a massive object heading his way, maybe a chunk of a wall or even a car. Flarence curled into a ball and decreased his weight. An instant later, the object struck him with enough force to knock him out of the wind current.

He tumbled high above the buildings as he was thrown from the tornado, soaring above the city with no sense of direction. It felt like forever before he finally felt solid ground, and in spite of his healing powers, the rubble that had pounded him, coupled with the long fall, hurt badly. After his bones popped back into place and his wounds closed, he realized he was on the lakefront, where the sand had made for a slightly more comfortable landing than if he fell on concrete. He turned to the city and saw the tornado in the distance, strong as ever, sucking up buildings as it moved. Apparently, Darren had not seen Flarence escape and was still trying to pummel him.

Flarence created his own tornado, sucking up water as it grew stronger over the lake. When it was complete, he pushed it toward Darren's storm. As his tornado moved, Flarence froze the water it sucked up to create massive blocks of ice, and heated the sand it collected while crossing the beach to create millions of glass shards.

Controlling the movement of a tornado was difficult, but Flarence moved it close enough to Darren's for the two to interact. Then he performed an astral projection. Though the spell was usually useless for tracking down other Genies, in this case he knew exactly where Darren was. His projection drifted through the city and found Darren standing in the eye of his tornado, a look of confusion on his face as it subsided. The real surprise was moments away.

DARREN

He couldn't guess how Flarence had done it, but the tornado he'd made was fading. Darren tried to manipulate the air around him to recreate his tornado, but it wasn't working. Whatever Flarence was doing was completely absorbing the energy of his storm.

Rubble crashed down all around him, but it wasn't just the bricks and metal he had collected in his tornado. Before he could summon his body away from the area, he felt a surge of blinding pain from glass shards. Ice fell as well, ranging in size from golf balls to small cars. Unable to focus on summoning, he threw his arms over his head and staggered through the falling wreckage, which seemed endless. He fell to his knees as his leg was crushed by a pile of bricks, and then he felt a crushing weight on his back. He was blinded, pinned, and in agonizing pain. He panicked as objects kept falling all around him, fearing that Flarence might be able to get the drop on him.

The crashing continued longer than Darren thought possible, but it did end, and he slowly crawled out of the pile of rubble. When he was free, he rolled onto his back and stared at the sky, shaken and battered but healing. He knew his current state made him vulnerable and that this moment was Flarence's best opportunity to attack, but his head, neck, back, arms, ribs, and legs all felt like they were on fire. He flexed his hands and toes a few times as the feeling returned and closed his eyes tightly for a moment to clear the dust from them.

When he opened his eyes, Flarence towered over him with the Stakehail Colt. Darren heard a click as the trigger was pulled, and he focused as best he could on the icicles erupting from the barrel. He guessed that waking up to the sight of a gun had given him an adrenaline boost that improved his magical abilities, because in spite of the lingering pain, he was able to melt all the icicles and felt only a splash of water on his face.

Still lying on his back, Darren swiped at Flarence's ankles with his saw blade. Flarence jumped back and avoided it, which gave Darren a chance to collect himself and get back on his feet. He still felt numb in places but was getting better. "You almost got me there," he said.

Flarence didn't respond or reload the Stakehail Colt. Instead, he tossed his gun away and advanced on Darren with his fists raised. Darren summoned the gun to his body, but as soon as it reached his hand, it turned to dust and Flarence threw a punch. Darren backed away and struggled to defend himself as Flarence lashed out with his Wrist Cannon. Darren tripped over something, flailing his arms to regain his balance and barely aware he had dropped his saw blade.

He swayed back and forth as he tried to stay on his feet, then started to feel light-headed. He fell to his hands and knees and tried to lift his head, but his body wouldn't cooperate. He felt pressure, rather than pain, as he fell onto his back. It took him a moment to realize he had been kicked in the ribs. His vision was blurry, and he could barely make out the image of Flarence standing over him with a smug grin.

"I did get you there," said Flarence as he reached into a suit pocket and took out an empty vial. "You didn't melt those icicles. I did, and there was more than just water in them. I mixed some of Soleil's poison into each shot. That's what's getting you."

"This won't hold me down forever," said Darren. He had survived Soleil's poisons before. He could do it again.

"No," said Flarence, "the poison probably won't kill you, but it'll hold you still long enough for me to do to you what you did to my dad."

Through the blurry vision and light-headedness, Darren realized that the saw blade was in Flarence's hand. The last thing he saw was his own weapon arcing toward his skull.

SOLEIL

The wind from the tornadoes subsided, which made it easier to focus on the chase. The Cannibal had run off when it heard the crashes of the crumbling buildings, and Roy had chased after it. Soleil was chasing Dr. Wicker, who was summoning his body to different places throughout the city. The moment Dr. Wicker arrived somewhere, he instantly shot himself again and summoned his body to another place in the distance just before Soleil could reach him.

Dr. Wicker raised his gun upward, summoned his body to the ledge of an apartment complex, and hoisted himself onto the roof. Soleil summoned his own body there and felt glad the pursuit was finally over. But the feeling was short-lived as Dr. Wicker fired a deconstruction spell at a water tower. Soleil altered the viscosity of the water as it rushed toward him, slowing its flow so that it slipped around his feet like syrup but did not carry him away. Dr. Wicker fired a freeze spell at the water around Soleil's feet and quickly summoned his body away. The pain from the frostbite broke Soleil's focus, and he was nearly thrown off the building as the water in the tower continued to gush out. He was trapped—frozen in place as the ice around his legs kept him glued to the roof—holding his breath and feeling like he was anchored to the bottom of a river. It didn't last long, but by the time all the water had passed, he had lost sight of Dr. Wicker.

Soleil melted the ice and went to the edge of the roof. He raced to all sides of the building, scanning the structures around him and the streets below. There was no sign of Dr. Wicker, and he decided that helping the people suffering down there was just as important as fighting. He stepped off the ledge and floated gracefully to the street. When he touched the ground, he saw a man crawling along the sidewalk. Soleil formed what closely resembled a leg brace out of the door of a nearby car and tied it to the man's leg with a section of seatbelt, then made him a walking stick out of the car's hood. He used his powers to free a man who was trapped under a pile of rubble, and saved someone else from being trampled. He saw a lot of people lying still and was going to check to see which were dead when he was tackled from behind and felt something sting his shoulder.

"Soleil!" It was Roy's voice. Soleil heard a thud and then the stinging in his shoulder was gone. When he rolled over, Roy was standing over him and the Cannibal was on its back. Now that he had been struck by the tip of the Cannibal's snake-like arm, he realized that the appendage was too thick and solid to be a stinger. It was as if Dr. Wicker had jammed a dog's tooth onto the end of the Cannibal's arm. Roy tried to help him up, but his fingers slipped on Soleil's wet poncho. "Sorry," said Roy, "I didn't know Genies could sweat so much."

"I'm not sweating. The Old Ticker tried to drown me."

The Cannibal was on its feet circling Roy and Soleil. It snapped its jaws and waved its clawed arm back and forth. As it did, its head jerked sporadically from side to side. "What's wrong with it?" asked Roy.

"I got it with a dart earlier," said Soleil. "The poison is making it hyperactive and giving it uncontrollable muscle contractions."

"Great, so it has trouble looking directly at us," said Roy. "That's not exactly a game changer."

"It's the best I could do, so try to make the most of it."

Then Dr. Wicker appeared, walking toward them confidently, holding his gun at waist level pointed at the ground. As he got closer, the Cannibal stopped pacing. Its head darted from Soleil to Roy to Dr. Wicker, who ignored it. "This is the end for both of you," said Dr. Wicker. "You thought killing me was difficult. Now you'll have to deal with me and my monster."

Hearing Dr. Wicker's confidence, Soleil saw his advantage. Dr. Wicker thought he had created an intelligent being, or at least an animal that would recognize and respect its master. But Soleil had realized that the Cannibal was rabid, built to attack, and would not recognize, let alone respond to, the person who had made it. The trick was making the monster attack its creator—before Dr. Wicker became aware he didn't have as much control over the situation as he thought.

"Stay here," Soleil said to Roy, "and don't move."

"You stay here," said Roy. "I'll snap his neck before he can raise his gun."

Before Roy could move, Soleil grabbed his sleeve. Roy seemed to consider running at Dr. Wicker regardless of what Soleil had said, but he relaxed and stood still. Soleil slowly stepped toward Dr. Wicker. In his peripheral vision, he could see that the Cannibal was on edge and shaking with tension. Soleil's plan was to coax Dr. Wicker into making the first move. His hand was positioned near a vial, and he twitched his finger. The Cannibal didn't attack but neither did Dr. Wicker, who continued to look at Soleil with his gun at his side.

"Enough of this," said Roy, who lost his patience and ran toward Dr. Wicker. The Cannibal, with its incredible reflexes and powerful legs, extended its snake-like arm to trip Roy, then pounced on him—just as Soleil had expected.

"Good boy!" shouted Dr. Wicker as he raised his gun and fired at Soleil, who jumped several feet in the air to avoid the spell. Then, when he was directly over Dr. Wicker, he increased his weight tenfold and fell to the ground hard and fast. Dr. Wicker dove to avoid the attack, and Soleil instantly pulled a vial out of his poncho. As he threw it, Dr. Wicker scrambled away, avoiding the poison but moving closer to Roy and the Cannibal.

Roy was right when he said the poison wasn't a game changer, but at least it made the Cannibal unstable. The beast was snarling more, and it pounded its clawed arm on the street as the fighting continued. After being punched by Roy, it didn't retaliate but arched its back and howled at the sky. Then it spun around a few times, flailing its upper limbs wildly, before lunging at a random person— who happened to be Dr. Wicker.

"What are you doing?" screamed Dr. Wicker. He frantically backed away and pointed at Soleil. "Him! Sic him!" The Cannibal didn't listen. Dr. Wicker turned his gun on his creation but was too slow. The Cannibal wrapped its snake arm around Dr. Wicker's wrist and pulled his hand to its mouth. It bit down hard on the weapon and wrenched it from his grasp, leaving a deep cut in Dr. Wicker's hand. Soleil relaxed a little, waiting for the Cannibal to finish the job, and was caught off guard when it lunged his way and body-slammed him.

Once again, Soleil was pinned to the ground, his thigh caught under a clawed foot. Dr. Wicker's bleeding hand was still gripped in the Cannibal's snake-like arm. Roy shouted Soleil's name and ran to help, but the Cannibal impaled him in the chest with his clawed arm and lifted him off the ground. They were all in pain now, but the Cannibal, with the gun still in its mouth, was shrieking the loudest. The beast's head was still jerking about as its frustration turned to rage. Instead of finishing anyone off, it just cried and thrashed its body.

Soleil was still pinned, the beast's foot changing position and stabbing him in a different place each time. Soleil noticed its snake arm shift as it tightened its grip on Dr. Wicker, whose wrist was now broken. Its clawed arm made a wide arc that threw Roy away from the group. The Cannibal bit down harder on the gun, puncturing the grip. Soleil struggled to break away but had to stop and cover his ears as the pitch of the Cannibal's shrieks increased.

He thought the sound would rupture his eardrums, but the noise gradually softened, along with the other sounds around him as well. Soleil no longer heard the screams of people in pain, the crackling of burning cars, or even the blowing wind. His vision clouded, and he felt as though he was floating. Am I dying? he thought as his world faded away. The Cannibal's attack had hurt but shouldn't have been enough to kill him. What was happening?

Everything around him disappeared. Roy, Dr. Wicker, and the Cannibal were simply gone, as was the city. Soleil no longer felt the ground below him or saw the sky above. He moved his hand to his back, trying to feel the street he was lying on, but there was only emptiness. There was no blinding light, nor was there an enveloping darkness. His entire world was now blank. It was as though he had been shrouded in mist.

He tried to sit up but had trouble moving his body. It was like gravity had ceased to exist. Steadily, reality came back. He felt a gentle breeze and saw a tree materialize in the distance, and the soft glow of the moon came into view above. He was briefly relieved, but panic took over as more shapes formed around him, many of them unfamiliar. There were no people he could see, but there were houses—strange houses that he was sure were not in Chicago. As he breathed, he could taste the air on his tongue, more humid than it had been a moment ago. By the time the new world had finished forming, he was freaking out. His pulse raced, sweat beaded on his face, and one thought repeated over and over in his head: Where am I?

FLARENCE

Everything was quiet now. What had once been a pristine research facility was barely recognizable. Some parts of the outer walls looked new while others were breaking down as if they had undergone decades of erosion in a matter of seconds. Federal agents stared dumfounded at the building that had been the headquarters of the mad doctor's experiment.

Using an astral projection, Flarence had watched the entire scene play out. Dr. Wicker stood in the center, with Broadsord, his hostage, tied to a chair. Flarence was no expert on Chi bosons, but from what he understood, the center was the most controlled position. Dr. Wicker had been transported to Chicago in the year 2008, while Broadsord, a meter away from the center, would arrive somewhere in Illinois between the years 2005 and 2011. The uncertainty increased exponentially with distance. Some equipment in the room could have been transported to the other side of the world hundreds of years in the past or future. Thankfully, the blast radius had not been very wide, and most of the time traveling was contained in the building.

Now, as the hostage negotiators and armed agents stood scratching their heads, Flarence paced around the empty room alone. He understood exactly what had happened. It was the start of the event that had taken his brother away long ago. After killing Darren Raleigh, he searched for Soleil but had been unable to find him. Eventually, he found Roy, who explained that the Cannibal had both Dr. Wicker and Soleil pinned when suddenly the air became wavy and the three of them vanished. Roy led Flarence to the spot where it had happened, which looked similar to the way the research facility looked now: Some parts of the street were shiny and new while others had crumbled to dust or disappeared.

For years, Flarence searched for his brother, using every detail Roy could give him. Flarence wanted to tell Tyrell right away, but killing Darren had left them not on speaking terms. The years passed quietly. Soleil's fate remained a mystery, but it seemed that the threats of the Old Ticker had ceased. Flarence remained consumed with the knowledge that his enemy would come back someday. A part of Flarence wanted to kill Emmanuel Wicker while he was young, but the years of waiting for the doctor to be born gave him time to decompress and consider the ramifications that would bring.

He decided not to interfere with the future. His lifespan overlapped with Dr. Wicker's, whom he stalked through childhood and into adulthood. He subscribed to scientific magazines and read every paper Dr. Wicker published. He followed the weaponized Chi tech scandal and spied on Dr. Wicker when he started the research that was funded secretly by General Broadsord. Now Dr. Wicker's research had reached its climax with the time travel experiment. All that was left was a ruined laboratory. Part of the lab's ceiling had disappeared, causing a cave-in. An exposed pipe spilled water onto the floor as Flarence kicked a piece of fallen plaster. Years of spying and studying Dr. Wicker's research had given him a deeper understanding of Chi bosons but no idea of how to reverse what happened to Soleil in the Anomaly. He pulled a phone out of his pocket to make a call but stopped when he realized he was no longer alone. Someone had materialized in the center of the room.

"Well I'll be damned," said Flarence. "There is such a thing as fate."

Dr. Wicker scrambled to his feet and looked around frantically. "This is my lab," he said as he stumbled toward an exit door that was now blocked by the collapsed ceiling. He tried to move some of the rubble, but his injured hand and wrist stopped him. He went toward another exit, but Flarence was standing in his way. Instinctively, Dr. Wicker reached for his holsters but found no weapons in them. "My guns," he shouted. "One of them was in the Bionuclear Beast's brain! The other was in its mouth!"

"For the moment, we're both unarmed," said Flarence, who had not yet drawn his weapons.

The two stared at each other for a moment, and Dr. Wicker calmed down. "My whole life, you knew what was going to happen," he said.

"It took me a while to piece it all together," said Flarence. "Roy told me what happened to you during the Anomaly. When your gun was damaged, the Chi generator was exposed."

"And the other generator I placed in the Bionuclear Beast's skull was active as well," said Dr. Wicker. "The energy from the two sources interacted. They became stronger and grew unstable."

"It became so unstable that it warped time," finished Flarence. "It resulted in a situation similar to the one you created here but much weaker. The blast radius only enveloped you, your monster, and my brother. It seems you boomeranged right back to where you started."

The color drained from Dr. Wicker's face. "If I'm back to the moment I left, that means the cops are still outside! You have to get me out of here. They'll kill me!"

"They aren't going to kill you," said Flarence. "I am."

"You don't mean that," said Dr. Wicker. "You need me alive. If you wanted to stop the Anomaly by killing me, you could have done it the day I was born."

"No I couldn't," said Flarence. "You don't understand what you've done. You called your monster the Bionuclear Beast, but my father had another name for it. Dad told us about a monster called the Cannibal which ran freely in ancient Egypt, terrorizing everyone and everything in its path until it was killed by a group of warriors. One of those warriors was Mohinaux, my father, who was affected by it before the killing blow was delivered. Dad described the Cannibal to Soleil and me before he died, and it had a striking resemblance to your Bionuclear Beast. So no, I couldn't kill you when you were born. I needed you to build the spellcasting revolvers, I needed you to bring them to the year 2008, I needed you to animate the Cannibal, and I needed the Cannibal to get sent back in time. If any of those events had been interrupted, my brother and I might never have been born."

"Let me help you get Soleil back," said Dr. Wicker. "Nobody knows more about Chi tech than me. There's got to be something I can do."

"I don't care," said Flarence. "I miss Soleil, but after all the people you've killed, I wouldn't spare your life even if you could find him."

"If what you've told me is true, then you owe me your life," said Dr. Wicker. "Besides, it's been nearly a hundred years since we last met. Do you even remember anyone I hurt?"

"All too well," said Flarence. He reached into the inner pocket of his jacket, which made Dr. Wicker flinch, but instead of removing the Stakehail Colt, he pulled out an old, worn scarf which he tied around his face. "Does this ring a bell? It belonged to the woman who got incapacitated by the juiced-up fly you made. That didn't kill her, by the way. She recovered and had a long and happy life. But it did change her. I didn't realize it at the time, but the moment she was hurt by that creature marked the end of our partnership. In fact, it was the beginning of the end of our friendship. For that, I put the blame entirely on you. So thanks for being responsible for my existence and for offering to help find my brother, but none of that makes up for driving me and Claire apart."

"You're still not going to kill me," said Dr. Wicker. "You talk a big game, but if I understand all this correctly, you don't need me anymore. Maybe you couldn't have killed me when I was born, but you could have killed me the second I arrived in this room. If you're angry enough to kill me, what are you waiting for?"

Flarence extended the hand that was holding his phone and displayed the time on the screen. It was 11:57. "This is too good to pass up." He summoned a piece of pipe to his body and caught it with his free hand.

Dr. Wicker's knees shook as he assessed the situation. He was unarmed, injured, trapped, and had less than a minute to live. "Flarence, please," he begged, "I really can help you find Soleil. Give me a chance at redemption. Maybe I can reverse everything I've done to you. Maybe I can even bring Claire back."

The clock advanced one minute, and Flarence let go of the phone. "Time of death: two minutes to midnight." He thrust the pipe like a spear into Dr. Wicker's chest.

TYRELL

"Tyrell Raleigh." The names were being read off in alphabetical order by last name, so he had been waiting a while. By the time the dean reached the R's, most of the people around him were bored and distracted, but he remained focused and excited. Receiving the engineering degree was more than just being handed a piece of paper. Graduating was his way of fulfilling his parents' wishes. He also wasn't going to be left hanging out to dry afterward. The previous day, he had gotten a job. There was still a lot of paperwork to get through, and from what the contact had told him, it sounded like his entry-level position would be far from exciting, but he wasn't complaining. Simply having a job was much more than could be said for most people in his graduating class. He beamed as he rolled his chair across the auditorium, glancing to the seats as he did, catching a glimpse of Claire as her camera flashed.

During the events in Chicago, Claire's injured leg had surprised the doctors, but lots of cleaning, painkillers, ointments, and rest had eventually resulted in an almost-complete recovery. Her leg was sore from time to time, and she wasn't as agile as she used to be, but she was still on her feet.

Flarence had also stopped by to visit once in a while, but most of his time was spent with Roy, who had become his new partner in crime fighting while Claire was incapacitated. Once Claire was able to walk and hop fences again, they asked her to join them, and for a brief period she did, but she had met a lot of new people while she was recovering. She started spending less time with Flarence and more time with Tyrell and his friends. Her scarf hung in her closet and had not been worn in months. When Flarence pleaded with her to help kill a giant worm shortly after the Anomaly, it sounded exciting, but she refused to tag along. Things had changed. She wasn't Razor Punk anymore.

An hour after Tyrell was awarded his degree, the ceremony ended. Only one graduate threw a hat in the air. Afterward, Tyrell went to celebrate with Claire and their friends Ben and John at a place that sold the cheapest drinks and greatest pizza on campus. It was still early in the afternoon, but it was also a special occasion, so nobody objected to splitting a pitcher of beer. They bought a pizza that was half pepperoni for Tyrell and Claire, who were meat lovers, and the other half topped with pepperoni, sausage, ham, and bacon for John and Ben, who were super-meat lovers.

"I heard back about one of the positions I applied for," Tyrell shouted over the talk and the television sports channel. "I got the job." There was a round of cheers, clinking glasses, and pats on the back. John asked for details. "It's a young company," Tyrell explained. "They were only established a little over a year ago and only have a few locations so far. They make detectors."

"You mean like metal detectors?" asked Ben.

"It's more complicated than that," said Tyrell. "One part of what they do is focused on development of particle counters. Most of their products are sold to universities and small labs, but they work with big names as well. They've sold devices to some of the big particle accelerators."

"What's the place called?" asked John.

"It's not the most creative name," said Tyrell. "It's called Sensor and Detector Technology, S&D for short." The three of them jumped as Claire dropped her glass. "Are you all right?"

"Yeah," said Claire, wiping the spilled beer with her sleeve, since her napkin was balled up and covered with grease and pizza sauce. "It just slipped. Congratulations, Tyrell. I'm really happy for you."

BROADSORD

He wasn't sure if he'd passed out or if his vision had temporarily been lost. The memories came in waves, and most of them felt like a dream. There had been a fight. He had been hurt. He was still hurting, which meant he was alive. The last thing he remembered was a series of crashes, and then everything faded. After that, he felt a gentle breeze on his face and woke up on the side of a road with fields of corn to his left and right. He couldn't remember what had happened, but thankfully, he was still dressed in his uniform and had all his possessions, including his wallet and phone. He called a friend.

When the ringing stopped, there was a brief pause and then a snapping sound. At first, Broadsord thought it was static but then realized it was chewing. " 'Lo?" said a high-pitched voice that sounded like it belonged to a young man with his mouth half-full of food. " 'oo dith?"

"I'm looking for George Coulder," said Broadsord. "Is he there?"

A slurping indicated the boy was washing down his food with a long drink. "Wrong number, man," he said.

Broadsord checked the screen. "No, this is the right number. I need to speak to George Coulder."

"Don't know whadda tell ya, man. No George here." The boy hung up. Broadsord called his other contacts, but nobody who answered was the person he expected. Panicking, he tried calling his wife, but again, he was told he had misdialed.

He activated his map app and headed for the closest town a few miles away. Sore and on foot, it took him a long time to get there. When he walked into a diner, the waitress greeted him with a smile, a menu, and a glass of water. He was so thirsty that as soon as she pulled the pitcher from the rim of his glass, Broadsord tried to drink it all in one go.

"Military man, huh," she said, noticing his uniform. Unwilling to take the water away from his lips, he settled for a nod. When the glass was empty, he set it down on the counter loudly to signal that he was finished, but the waitress did not return to refill it. The smile she'd had when he walked in was gone. She had her elbows on the counter and was leaning over her phone tapping the screen with a finger. Apparently, she wasn't going to talk to him if he wasn't going to talk to her. Until he figured out what was wrong with his phone and got hold of someone he knew, he might as well try to be friendly.

"I'm sorry," he said as he rose from the stool and approached the waitress. "I'm usually more talkative, but it's been kind of a long day. Do you want me to take a look at that?"

"You wanna look at my phone? Why?"

"I saw you were tapping at the screen. I figured it was broken."

She tapped the screen one last time and the phone made a high-pitched beep. "It's called text messaging."

"With your fingers?" said Broadsord.

The waitress gave him a strange look. He imagined that his expression was similar. She held the phone up, giving him a clear view of the screen. "Haven't you ever seen a phone before?"

The phone was huge. He had noticed that the moment he saw it and taken it to be an old model. Now that he saw the screen, he realized it was ancient. The glass was cluttered with icons with labels underneath. Surely, this woman didn't have to tap each image to activate the apps. Broadsord's eyes drifted around the screen and then rested on the upper left corner, where the time and date were displayed. His hands struck the counter, and he nearly fell out of his seat.

The waitress backed away and looked at him with wide eyes. Broadsord ran out of the diner and kept going until he was alone again on the deserted road. The experiment had actually worked. Manny Wicker had distorted time, and he had been caught in the blast.

He pulled his phone out of his pocket and held it close to his mouth. "Search app," he said, making a blank bar and blinking line appear on the screen. At least he had been transported to a year that had internet. Unsure of where to start, he said "current events" but was greeted by a surge of results with no useful information. He took a moment to remember his confrontation with Dr. Wicker and recalled a word that kept coming up.

"Anomaly, early twenty-first century." The definition appeared on the screen. He nodded. The phone registered his movement and showed the next page of results. There was a list of headlines with the word anomaly, most of them published in 2008 and 2009. Broadsord looked at the links. The phone tracked his eye movements, and when he blinked twice, the content downloaded. He skimmed through articles describing the destruction and death toll of a catastrophe in Chicago. One article in particular caught his eye. It was about a man named Jethro Broadsord.

Broadsord read about his distant ancestor. He'd had a reputation for ranting about the Anomaly being caused by monsters with magical powers. Based on the articles, it didn't seem like a lot of people paid his story any mind. Broadsord found a web page where Jethro blogged about things he had seen before the Anomaly. Most of it told of Genies and a zombie. The only believable part was a description of a man dressed in black with a pair of spellcasting revolvers. It confirmed that Dr. Wicker had in fact been in Chicago. If there was the slightest chance of returning to his time, the key was finding Dr. Wicker, and the only lead Broadsord had was Jethro.

He checked his wallet. His debit card was useless, since his bank account had not been set up yet, which meant he would have to get to Chicago with whatever cash he had. He hoped it was enough, and that once he was there, he'd be able to find his crazy relative.

JOCELYN

She approached the truck that had several cases of water bottles. It was amazing how many people had volunteered to clean up in the aftermath of the disaster. A lot of work had been done in the past three years, although it would take much longer to completely rebuild. For a while, Jocelyn Roux spent most of her time with volunteer groups cleaning up the streets. Several months were spent digging graves for the scores of fallen civilians. She also worked with cleanup crews who sorted scraps of metal, bricks, and plastic for others to decide what was salvageable. Once there was no more rubble to remove, she stayed busy with other projects focused on recovering from the Anomaly. While the work felt good, she was really there to get information from the other volunteers.

At the moment, she was helping prepare lunch boxes for construction workers. The sky was overcast. She wore a green raincoat and black sweatpants, plain clothes that contrasted with her flashy jewelry. She had no piercings but wore four bracelets on each wrist and a ring on each finger. On her left hand, all the rings were bands, but on the right, each was embedded with a different jewel.

"Four more cases of water," she said to someone standing by the truck taking an inventory of its contents. In addition to the water bottles, the truck was packed with cardboard boxes containing sandwiches, fruit, and potato chips.

"That's all we need for this one," the man said as he raised his clipboard and scribbled on the record sheet. "Are you going to stick around and help assemble the afternoon load?"

"Definitely," said Jocelyn. "It wouldn't feel right to slow down when there's still so much more to do. Were you in the city when it happened?"

"I wasn't in the heat of it. My uncle was there. He was crushed when an apartment fell. Phil, the guy who's driving this truck later, experienced it up close."

Jocelyn waited until a man with a prosthetic leg wobbled toward the truck and pulled a set of keys from his pocket. "I take it you're Phil," she said. "I was wondering if you'd tell me about what you saw during the Anomaly. I heard you were there."

Phil opened the truck door and struggled into the seat. "Hop in. I'll tell ya 'bout it on the way. Besides, I could use some help distributin' the lunches when I get there." Jocelyn got into the passenger's seat as he put the keys in the ignition. The old truck sputtered, but Phil got it started and slowly guided it onto the street. "It's when I lost my leg. I don't know how ta explain what I saw. I ran as fast as I could, even though I didn't know if there was anyplace safe ta go. Then something hit my leg. Couldn't run after that, so I crawled as fast as I could. Someone saw me. It was a guy wearing what looked like a blanket. Sorta like a coat without sleeves."

"A poncho?" said Jocelyn.

"I guess. I don't know much in the way of fashion lingo. The guy wearing it, he saw me struggling and made me a brace and a walking stick. Just tore chunks of metal off a car and molded it inta new shapes. Almost looked like he was doing it with his mind. He was an angel. That's the only explanation I can think of." He took his eyes off the road for a moment to look hard at Jocelyn's face. "Most people start smirking when I tell 'em that, think I was seeing things 'cause of the pain and shock."

"Maybe you were," Jocelyn said sweetly, "but ever since the Anomaly, I've decided to start believing in miracles."

As she went on with her volunteer work, Jocelyn continued to press for more information about the man in the poncho. When she'd heard about the Anomaly, she was positive that Mohinaux or her children had something to do with it, and traveled to America to search for them.

It had taken years of questioning random survivors, but she finally found confirmation that one of her sons had been present during the Anomaly. Not only was he there, but the man spoke of him like a hero. With any luck, it wouldn't be much longer before she found both of them. She hoped to find Mohinaux as well, so she could give him a piece of her mind for running off with them in the first place.

ABOUT THE AUTHOR

Hugh Fritz is a fan of monsters, mad scientists, sorcerers, and anything that involves beings with incredible powers beating each other senseless. After years of writing research papers, he decided it was time to give reality a rest and let his imagination run wild. This is his first book, and it has been an illuminating experience making the transition from reader to author.

He was born in Chicago where he spent most of his life until moving to the Southwest five years ago. He finds inspiration bouncing ideas off other novelists in a critique group, but hours of television and finding the right songs to put him in the writing mood play an important role as well. He is currently working on the final installment of the Mystic Rampage series, so be on the lookout for the conclusion.

ABOUT THE ILLUSTRATOR

Lothar Speer heralds from Southern Germany's Black Forest. As a classically trained artist he studied at Vienna's National Academy of The Fine Arts and received his MFA from Philadelphia's Pennsylvania Academy of Fine Arts. As an award-winning fine artist and illustrator he relishes in collaborating with writers to bring never-seen worlds to life, to celebrate flights of fancy, and the epic magic of human imagination.

His website is RenProject.com.